The Good Citizen

by

Joël Henning Doty

Four Wise Monkeys Publishing
St. Louis, MO

There's something happening here
What it is ain't exactly clear
There's a man with a gun over there
Telling me I got to beware

I think it's time we stop, children, what's that sound
Everybody look what's going down

The Good Citizen

Jenny

Even though I'm early, there are hundreds of kids jammed in front of the school, so I'm forced to stand in the very back of the crowd, near the street, squashed between a boy with greasy hair who slurps handfuls of granola into his mouth and a girl who has B.O. I can barely move, but I don't care.

There's only one Protector Day in a thirteen-year-old citizen's life, and I don't want to miss a minute of it!

The enormous Broadcaster screen hanging over the school entrance shows a woman smiling and waving her yellow Protector. A man in a Buy Now shirt shakes her hand, and the Broadcaster speakers blare out:

Thank you, Cathy Nichols, for shooting the would-be troublemaker in your neighborhood. You got your Protector at Buy Now.

"Quiet!" some kid yells to the crowd as a picture of another Protector shows on the screen. It might be the new kind that uses laser beams, not bullets.

Buy Now has the latest Protector designs on sale.

"Splitting Souls?!" a bunch of us yell at the Broadcaster as if it will hear our demand. We want an update on the Protector model featuring the Splitting Souls band's photos. It's the most popular model for teens this year and on back order. The Broadcaster always announces the Protectors in stock. No Splitting Souls this morning, I guess. The Broadcaster, like all the others around town, just continues with usual news, videos and information citizens have uploaded.

Sunshine all day. I bought candy from the vending machine, but it doesn't taste good. How do I send it back? On time students make on-time employees.

I get a whiff of the girl's B.O. again. Is she from an opportunity family and never got the rules on hygiene? I start to move away when the greasy-haired kid elbows me. "Look at the freaks," he says.

I turn and see six people in the middle of the street. They hold signs that read: No Protectors, No Parade, and Close the Homesteads.

"Harmless protesters," I tell the boy. *They're easy to ignore*, I think. Unlike stench girl. Small groups like this show up every year around parade time. My mom says protesters will complain about anything, and ignoring them is the best way to make them disappear. She should know. She's the safety officer for Middletown, and one day I plan to be her partner.

The protesters chant as they move closer.

"Tomorrow I'll have a Protector," the boy says as he pretends to point one at one of the protesters.

"And if you use it tomorrow, I'll report you to the safety office," I say back.

"Shoot to kill," the boy says as he continues to point his finger.

"Shoot to stop," I correct, feeling my cheeks get warm. I hate it when people can't understand the laws. "Protect yourself; protect your property; protect community property; protect your friends, family, and fellow citizens," I quote from the rulebook. "None of those apply to protesters."

"What do you know?"

"I know that in four weeks I'll start at the Safety Officer Academy," I say looking him straight in the eye. I don't add that I still have a few qualification requirements to complete, but my exam was the big one. Last week – on my third and last chance – I PASSED! I screamed so loud my mom thought I would break a glass. But she was happy. I did fine on the body-target shooting section, but I'm not the best on multiple-choice tests with answers like "all the above." Why can't it just be yes or no? Right or wrong? Now I just have to pass math and finish community service. The bell rings and kids push and shove into the building. I glance again at the protesters.

Opportunity people – not citizens.

I can tell because of the red H on their shirts. They live in the Homesteads operated by Governcorp. Why carry a Close the Homesteads sign? Where would they live? They would be deported, for sure. Besides, why protest something fun like a parade with cool floats and bands? And why would anyone not want a Protector to keep safe? It's part of being a good citizen.

As the group passes the viewer hidden in the trees, I jump at the sudden blare of the warning siren and cover my ears. Someone in the group must be a lawbreaker spotted by the viewer camera. Comfort Center vans screech around the corner. The protesters run, but the officials in the red, white, and black uniforms jump out of the vans and squirt them with the stun medicine from their peace wands. The six protesters collapse to the ground and are loaded into the vans in record time. The sirens turn off. Wow. I'd consider that job if I hadn't already decided on safety officer.

I file into school, scanning the crowd for Jade. I need the math homework answers from her before the assembly. Passing algebra is a stupid qualification to get into the academy.

I get to the locker area at the same time as Russell Murray.

"I've just been attacked, crushed, and man-handled by hordes of zombies." He collapses against the locker next to me, and I snort a laugh. Ever since kindergarten, Russell has been next to me or behind me—his last name, Murray, comes right after mine, Morgan. He's the only person I know with hair as curly as mine, but his is short and, lucky for him, coal black and not red. He's big enough to be a football player, but when his glasses fall off, and his books drop, I'm reminded of why the team hasn't invited him. I pick up some of his books.

"Thanks." He fixes his glasses and opens his locker. "I hate assembly days."

"You can't hate *this* assembly," I say. "Have you picked out a Protector?"

"The chrome model that just came out has the periodic table on the right side and unsolved theorems on the other," Russell says. "I'd like it better if it was a cover."

"Doesn't it seem we've waited forever to get our Protectors?" I ask.

"If I were a thirteen-year-old, fifty-pound dog, instead of a thirteen-year-old boy, I'd have waited more than a lifetime. But I've actually waited probably only one seventh of my total life span."

As usual, I'm not sure what Russell is talking about.

"Did you see the protesters?" Russell asks.

"The Comfort Center officials showed up super fast."

"I don't think they should have gone to the Comfort Center," Russell says.

"Why not?" I ask.

"I doubt they all did something illegal."

"Well they all looked the same, and they were together," I say.

"That's not much evidence."

"A lawful society is a peaceful society."

"Things happen at the Comfort Center."

"The Comfort Center rejuvenates and restores minds to health," I say.

"That's from the Broadcaster."

"Yep," I nod with a grin. "Responsibility for the law starts with each person."

"Why do you...?"

An announcement over the speaker interrupts. "All students who have volunteered to be a buddy report to auditorium door two. Buddy volunteers, door two."

I turn to Russell. "What? Does she mean now? On Protector Day?"

"Sounds like it," he replies. "Do you have a buddy?"

I don't want him to think I'm stuck with the job. "Yes," I say. "Of course. Community service builds character and leadership skills."

He shakes his head and sighs. "That's from the Broadcaster, too," he says.

"Being a responsible helper is important," I add. I don't mention that I need to be a buddy to finish my credits.

Russell continues. "I don't feel competent with my social skills to mentor a new student who has just become a citizen," he says. "Volunteering to be a buddy to an opportunity person is very commendable."

I want to laugh at Russell's adult tone, but he looks so sincere that I smile and shrug instead.

"You have a personable disposition and a really nice smile," he says. "You'll be good at it."

"Thanks, Russell." If another guy had said this stuff, I'd either blush or think he was crazy; but Russell is Russell. He's comfortable with books, a respond-pad, microgames, and talking to me.

And he's right. I will be good at this job. I have no choice but to do it right. "Success today means a brighter future tomorrow." The Broadcaster doesn't need to remind me of that. I want to be the best safety officer in the whole country.

Russell keeps talking about the people with signs, and I don't even think he notices that I'm not listening.

"You're smart, Russell," I interrupt when he finally takes a breath. "Maybe you can find another way to help some new citizen," I say.

He smiles and looks down at his shoes. "Maybe," he mumbles.

I spot Jade down the hall with Trix and Sable, and I grab my stuff and run to catch up.

"You didn't stop at my locker," I say to Jade.

"Oopsie." She makes her lips form a circle and tilts her head like she's talking baby talk. "Guess you won't be sitting with us. Have you seen your 'buddy'?" She air-quotes. She does that a lot. Maybe that's what makes her cool, but sometimes it bothers me. Like now.

"No," I answer.

Jade is the most envied girl in our level—one of The Developers. She looks like a fashion model—much taller than me, but who isn't if you're five foot four? She's wearing a tight, red dress that shows off her boobs, and she has matching bing shoes with pointed toes and beautiful ribbons that go up to her knees. Her hair is even in a fancy twist like she's ready for prom.

"Bet you get a geek boy who doesn't talk English," Trix says. She holds her nose and pokes Jade as she laughs. "Some nerd who smells." I force myself to join in the laughter and not think of the girl I smelled earlier.

"Today was red day, Jenny." Jade holds up a math plug-in for my respond-pad but doesn't give it to me. The three of them join arms and stare at me. Sable's dress is new and tight-fitting just like Jade's. All their parents work for Governcorp headquarters.

I look down at my not-so-tight blue shirt and jeans and wish I had more of a lot of things.

"Oh. Totally forgot. Sorry." I smile a little and shrug.

I want to remind Jade that I don't own anything red because it clashes with red hair, but instead I say, "You look really glam."

Jade twirls around, modeling, and then hands me the plug-in. "I don't like it when anyone in the group forgets the plan."

"Buddy volunteers report to auditorium door two," the voice on the loudspeaker says again.

"Have fun with that," Jade says, and the three of them start toward the assembly. No way can I let them sit together and joke and laugh without me. Some 'buddy' I don't even know, is not going to wreck the best day of my life.

"Save me a seat," I say. "I'll meet you in a sec."

I sprint toward door two. I'll just find out who my buddy is and meet him or her later.

The line at the door is long and moves as slow as a security checkpoint. A girl from science class stands next to me bobbing her head. "Do you think World Disaster will play in the parade this year?" she shouts. She takes off her music muffs, and I can hear the popular band's beat. "Maybe they'll even be on our float," she says.

"That would be crazy," I say. "Riding on the float will be a heart attack."

I bob my head to the music and think how cool parade day will be. I'll be on the Safety Academy float and have my Splitting Souls Protector. I bet Jade will be jealous. I'll wear the blue safety officer uniform, which *goes* with red hair.

"I squeaked by on that body target with thirty percent," the girl says.

"Thirty percent is passing?" I ask.

"They just want you to be able to hit something."

If you can't hit a target in the red zone, go back to the field and practice, I think. There's no way the Academy accepts such a low rating! I don't remember seeing her at any of the exam sessions.

"You applied to the Academy?" I ask.

"Huh?"

"You said you were going to be on the float…"

"Yeah. We all are. The Opportunity float, with our buddies."

"What?" I say as I'm bumped into the volunteer table.

"Name?" a teacher asks.

"There must be some mistake."

"I wouldn't know unless you tell me your name," she says.

"I'm going to the Academy and…"

"Name?"

"Oh. Jenny Morgan."

"Morgan…Morgan…here it is. No mistake. Row one."

"There's a mix-up with…"

"Next."

She hands me a folder and the seat assignment and then waves me aside for the next person. Jade would be able to think of something sarcastic or funny to say, but I just stand there and read my buddy's name: Hannah Cossack.

The person I need to get rid of before all my plans are ruined.

Hannah

"My turn."
"No, it's my turn."

I fix toast as I watch my twin sisters, Emma and Lily, argue about folding their bed back into a sofa. They love to watch it appear and disappear. They seem to wonder if it's there even when you can't see it. They've opened and shut it a million times this morning, and the only good thing about their noise is that it blocks out some of the Broadcaster's chatter. The incessant voice!

Your news. Your way. This is Middletown getting the news out fast, first, and free. This is Charlotte, and I love the results of my new kale diet.

I glance at the screen, and instead of a seeing a slim Charlotte, the Broadcaster shows dogs playing in a field. Images and sound are often out of synch. Twenty-four hours a day, people in the community, businesses, or Governcorp sends in messages, ads, or information. We can turn it off, but if an official Governcorp message is broadcasted, the machine automatically comes back on. Official messages are frequent, so it's easier to leave our home Broadcaster on and at a low volume.

Transit line ninety-four closed for repairs at midnight. Mango flavored cough drops are good. I can't find my keys. Where are they? The penguins like to swim at the zoo, but the monkeys hide in the trees and scream. What's not to like?

"What's not to like?" My dad tickles Emma and Lily, and they laugh and roll on the bed.

"Let's go, girls." My mom maneuvers around two big moving boxes. She has new ribbons and a hairbrush in her hand.

"Hannah, Hannah." Emma takes the ribbon from my mom and rushes over to me. I'm glad they have something new today. My dad says we'll be able to afford more things now that we're citizens. I put Emma's hair in a ponytail, and then do Lily's to match.

"Bye, Hannah." Lily hugs me first, and then Emma joins in. New friends and a new school will be a lot easier at age four, than at age fifteen.

I smile and tease, "Don't kiss any boys on your first day unless they're really cute."

Emma sticks out her tongue, and Lily copies, making me laugh.

My mom shoos them out the door and asks my dad to watch them a minute. She pours me some tea. "How did you sleep?"

I put jam on my toast instead of answering. Since moving, I've had nightmares.

"Maybe you won't find the school so terrible," she says.

I concentrate on spreading the jam evenly. Any school without my friends will be terrible.

"Well, don't kiss any boys unless they are really cute."

I can't help but smile. My mom hugs me and then goes out the door.

I chew my toast and hope my stomach can forget my nerves for once. I look out the window and think about fresh air and focus on things in the distance as if I'm fighting seasickness. If only I were on a ship and could fix everything by just staring at the horizon or, better yet, jumping off.

I've had the dream many times. *The monkey holds my hand and leads me to a tree loaded with bananas. I jump easily to a branch and begin to climb. With every stretch of my arm or leg, the tree grows and grows, and I'm climbing through the clouds, and I feel light and free. The monkey finds the perfect bananas for us. We rest on a branch in the quiet and eat. It's so peaceful. We joke and laugh, but then suddenly the sky turns black, and a huge cloud speeds toward us blaring, "Monkeys belong in the zoo! Monkeys not in the zoo will be arrested! Monkeys with girls will be shot!" I grab the tree branch and the monkey's hand to keep him safe, but the cloud has already taken him. As soon as he disappears, a shot rings out, and blood pours from the cloud like rain.*

Then I wake up.

This morning I could have sworn I saw a monkey tail outside my window.

"You ready, Hannah?" The excitement in my dad's voice is palpable as he comes into the kitchen.

"Almost," I say. *Never*, I think.

"I'll drive you," he offers.

"You don't have to."

"Parents should drive on the first day," he says with conviction. I shake my head, but he keeps trying. "You look nice," he says.

"Thanks."

"Nicer if you'd smile," he teases. "Did you see how giddy Lily and Emma were?"

I want to remind my dad that my little sisters get excited about anything new, but instead, I just sigh and say, "*Giddy* is a funny word."

"Giddy is how I feel about being a citizen," he says. "How you should feel too. Our struggle is over." I give him a smile because I know how important all this is to him.

The Broadcaster sounds again. I watch a woman blow out candles on a cake while the broadcaster voice describes someone's fun bus ride.

I turn the volume as low as possible without muting it. "I thought the Broadcaster would be less obnoxious in the citizen community," I say.

"Everyone needs to be informed," my dad replies.

"About the birthday cake or where to go on a bus?"

"Freedom of speech is a wonderful thing," my dad says emphasizing each word. "Never take it for granted."

I nod to appease him. My mom told me that years ago people known as "reporters" had jobs to research and disperse truthful information. That would have been an interesting job: to analyze things and find the facts.

The shirt you want is on sale at Murphy's.

The sound and pictures for ads are always in sync. They mesmerize.

I glance up at the screen to see men and women of every shape modeling an ugly brown-and-green shirt. The people smile and wave as though they are my friends. The Broadcaster tells us to use a speedy pass to order now, and we can pick up this fantastic outfit in just thirty minutes at Murphy's. A teenager in the ad touches the screen, and all her information is processed. She smiles as she picks up her new shirt.

Even I feel tempted.

"Now that we don't have to pay Homestead taxes, you can shop for some fab things, huh?" My dad has been watching, too.

"Never use the word *fab*, Dad. Never." He tries to tickle me, but I jump away fast, and we both laugh.

"That's the smile I love," he says. "Think of all we can enjoy now."

I do have my own room, and we no longer share a kitchen or bathroom with others. I nod again.

He seems satisfied and says, "Meet you in the car."

I think about my dream. I always feel so free before the nightmare part. I wish I could just skip school, go to the zoo, and watch the monkeys. It's my favorite place to think.

Official Report: The parade route will be posted next week.

I jump with the change in tone. Official announcements are designed to be forceful to make people literally stop and listen. The parade? I hate the parade. All people who live in the Homestead hate the celebration of the law that created it. Even though we moved out and now I'm a citizen, I can't change my mind as quickly as my dad has.

City schools and Governcorp join forces to provide more Protector training.

I also hate Protectors. I'm not a psychologist, but I know the pain in my stomach, and probably the nightmares are about the Protector law. Every citizen fourteen and over must carry one. We can qualify at thirteen. I thought about failing the qualifying tests on purpose, but my friend Kyle did that, and they just made him go every weekend to the body-target range and gave him respond-pad quizzes every night and, well...he told me not to torture myself. Could I ever use a Protector? Even if someone were attacking me? I think I would just run. Citizens are told to aim for legs, but no one in authority asks questions when a bullet goes astray–especially when it hits a person in the Homestead.

The Broadcaster wishes every good citizen a safe and happy day. I slam the door on the way out.

***

At school, I wait in a room with the other new citizen transfer students from the Homestead. We're easy to spot. Faded Governcorp-issue shirts limply hang on too thin shoulders or stretch on stomachs full of salt and sugar. Most kids have cut out the H symbol, leaving small holes that make them look even more impoverished. My mom and I are good with alterations, and though my secondhand clothes may not be high fashion, at least they fit.

The principal, Mr. Marshall, gives us locker numbers and codes and tells us how we will soon blend right in with citizen kids. Right.

"You are all Developers," he says. "We have no grade numbers here."

Students mumble to each other because we know we'll be in classes with kids much younger. It's assumed we are all behind. My mom's a teacher, so my sisters and I do fine, but there are no exceptions.

"I'm sure you'll all benefit from your studies, and after two years, you will move to the Decider level. As a Decider, you will choose a career path. When you graduate, you go on to college or a work environment, depending on your interests." He makes it all sound simple and logical.

The boy behind me whispers, "They give you a job or make you study something Governcorp needs. The only way you choose anything is if you're rich or know some high-up executive." I wonder if he's right.

The principal continues. "We have a buddy system here. All of you will have a citizen buddy for the next four weeks."

"Those buddies?" It's the boy behind me again. "They keep track of you for Governcorp." I turn to look at him. He has on a strange black shirt with white squiggle designs.

"Shut-up, A-hole," a girl in torn sweatpants says. "Do you want the viewers to send you to the Comfort Center on the first day?"

I feel sudden goose bumps, and I cross my arms. The Comfort Center.

The girl sees me looking at the boy's odd shirt, and she pulls a sweatshirt from her backpack.

"Make yourself presentable," she says. The boy pulls it on. "Brothers, right?" She looks at me and shrugs.

"Morning, Mr. Marshall," a loud, disembodied voice says. "Assembly is starting," the voice speaks again. I look around and see the small, black circle high on the wall; a person is watching and speaking from the office. It reminds me of all the hidden safety viewers in Middletown; the viewers everywhere in all the cities. The safety office watches all the streets and public build-ings, including the schools and Homesteads. Governcorp says the viewers eliminate crime so everyone can walk the streets without fear. Viewers save lots of money too because fewer officers are needed. Kyle says the real purpose is to spy on everyone. The goose bumps take over again, and I can't stop a shiver.

Mr. Marshall leads the group to the auditorium, where I take my seat, pull out a notebook, close my eyes, and breathe.

"Taking a nap?"

It's easy to recognize Kyle's voice. We're friends from the Homestead, and even though he gained citizenship, he visits the Homestead twice per month, like Governcorp allows.

"It would be nice to sleep through all this," I say without opening my eyes.

"You'll be okay," he says as he plops down into the seat next to me.

I sit up, smile, and hug him, hoping his confidence will rub off. "Promise?" I ask.

"There's a group of us meeting soon. You can come."

"Meeting about what?"

"This. Today. Everything."

"I can't."

"You can. You should." Kyle nods toward the front. "Look at that."

The red-and-black Governcorp logo is lit on the podium on stage. Four hands joined in a circle to represent technology, government, citizens, and business.

"The hands around our necks," Kyle says with a loud voice.

"Kyle," I warn, glancing around, but no one seems to be pay-ing attention to us.

"You're a citizen now, but never forget," he says.

How could I forget being moved from our nice house to the Homestead? I was five when the Ultimate Compromise hap-pened. Government became dysfunctional and went broke, so businesses united to form Governcorp and took over everything from schools to law enforcement. Lack of jobs and crime was blamed on immigrants, so Governcorp convinced politicians to redefine citizenship and build communities called homesteads for non-citizens. Anyone with a family member not born in this country—going back three generations—would be considered a non-citizen and labeled an "opportunity" person. My dad was born in the Ukraine, so we were no longer considered citizens. Families like ours had to either move to homesteads and pay high taxes or be deported. At the same time, laws gave citizens more rights to use Protectors to stop crime. Building homesteads and viewers and Broadcasters gave citizens jobs for the first time in years, and the high taxes made Governcorp officials wealthy. So, the homesteads became permanent.

Will I ever consider myself a citizen like my dad does? Kyle has been a citizen for two years, but he still thinks of himself as an opportunity person first. He's worked ever since I can remember and has been on his own way too long for someone his age. His parents died in a terrible Homestead building fire. The building had no sprinklers or smoke detectors. Governcorp said he couldn't stay in the country as an orphan, but he researched the law and found a loophole, and then he paid the citizenship taxes for himself. He'll be a great lawyer one day.

The principal announces that everyone must be seated, and Kyle goes back to his section. *Must I sit through a celebration of Protector use? Maybe I could sneak out?* I think about it for a minute until I turn over my notebook and see the sticky note: *I count on you to follow the rules. Love, Dad.*

Jenny

The auditorium is buzzing with students. I glance over to the Decider section– where the older students sit. HE'S in a seat on the aisle. I spot Jade and the others, but I'll have to walk right past him—unless I go all the way across the back and down the other side, and that's impossible with all these people.

Kyle is smart and dresses kind of plain, but like someone who can be plain on the outside and unique on the inside. I'm not sure that makes sense, but he's not like other boys. I mean, he looks like other boys. He has brown hair and wears it kind of old-fashioned, so part of it falls on his forehead, and sometimes he has to push it out of his eyes. But would another teenage boy bother to climb a rusty old fence to get a soccer ball for some little kids? He does nice things, but never shows off.

The guys in his row laugh and joke, but Kyle just stares at the auditorium stage. Wonder what he's thinking? I know he's on the debate team. Maybe he's planning his next argument.

Why do I look so horrible today? I should have put on a dress. Why didn't I save my allowance for a padded bra? I start down the aisle, trying to go as quickly as I can past Kyle, but other students aren't in a rush. Kids gather to talk, blocking the path, and I must weave around them. Someone knocks my arm and my respond-pad slips from my sweaty hand and lands near Kyle's row. Before I can think of escape, he picks it up and looks to see who dropped it. He stands up right in front of me. I feel my cheeks turn hot as we look at each other. Is it my imagination, or does he blush too?

"Yours?" he asks.

Please let my voice work, God. Please.

"Yeah. Thanks."

He smiles and hands it to me. His eyes are turquoise blue. If we ever slow dance, he'll be the perfect height for me in high-heeled shoes.

"Thanks." I smile back. Why can't I think of anything else to say?

"Your name's Jenny, right?"

He knows my name? He actually knows my name?

"Yeah." What's wrong with my brain?

"You got a perfect score on respond-pad programming."

He smiles again and my mind zeros out. "Oh. Yeah, I guess."

"It was in the weekly school announcements," he explains. "That's hard to do." His blue eyes light up, and he smiles. "Really hard."

The principal makes another announcement, and the crowd in front of me moves.

"See you around, Jenny."

"Yeah."

Somehow my legs and feet remember how to move forward because all I can think about is how many times I said "Yeah" and nothing else. Yeah, yeah, yeah! I head for Jade's row.

A teacher touches my arm. "Excuse me," she says, pointing to my buddy packet. "This is the buddy row."

I start to argue, but the lights dim, and she stands firm and points to an empty seat. Jade and the others laugh and wave at me. My seat is in the middle, and next to my empty chair is a girl bent over at the waist. Is she about to barf? Seriously? I'm not with my friends, I just ruined my chance with the one boy I like, and now I have to sit next to some weirdo. If my mom waves from the stage, I'll barf too.

Hannah

A girl with long, curly, auburn hair moves down my row. She looks mad or annoyed. *My buddy?*

My stomach churns. Breathe. Breathe. I can't throw up. I can't.

Music plays, and a woman in a safety officer uniform jogs down the aisle toward the stage. I sit up. I'll be okay. I just want to get this over with.

Everyone claps and cheers as the officer hops on the stage. She looks up and down the first few rows of kids and waves toward the girl next to me, but the girl pretends not to notice.

"Thank you. Wow. Thanks," the officer says. "I know lots of you are old pros at this, but new Developers...where are the new Developers?"

Everyone around me raises a hand, but I don't bother. We're all seated in the same area. I know a rhetorical question when I hear one.

The officer continues in her enthusiastic tone. "Your accuracy scores on the body targets were fantastic. And your written tests? The highest ever on the laws and regulations. Give yourself a hand."

The kids in the auditorium go wild. Most of the boys knuckle pound. The officer signals for everyone to quiet down and a screen lowers from the ceiling for the presentation. I close my eyes. I hear *oohs* and *aahs* and more clapping. The girl next to me bumps my elbow and with a start, I open my eyes. But the girl isn't concerned with me. She leans forward to give her full attention to the screen.

It was just an accidental bump.

The girl bounces in her chair, and her green eyes sparkle. Her round face has just a few freckles to make it interesting and pretty, and she glows with excitement. I almost moan when the word *giddy* comes into my head.

I look up at the screen. There are pictures of every type of Protector on the market. All are small enough to fit in a pocket. Many are the newest and most expensive kind, which injure or kill without drawing blood. I've heard the ads: Effective but not messy. No bullets needed. Protect yourself. Protect your friends. Protect your law.

"Your parents will be glad to know that Protectors will be a bargain this month to celebrate the anniversary of the Homestead and Citizenship law; red or blue, striped or plaid, teddy bear designs, horses…you name it." The officer smiles as if describing all the flavors of ice cream we can choose.

I'm transfixed as the slide show plays. First, a mother takes proper measurement of a girl's hand and arm. They smile. Next, the girl squeezes the trigger. Her mother cheers as the girl hits a cardboard target.

"Have your parents measure your hand, your arm length, and your strength before buying a Protector for you," the officer says.

Breathe.

"Any questions from you, new students?"

A new citizen boy raises his hand and asks if it's okay to use a hand-me-down model if his brother is bigger than he is. Another girl asks if there are special models for left-handed people. With each question, the students around me get more excited and chatty about what kind and color each will get and where to shop.

"Remember, accidents happen when you have not been properly fitted."

What does that even mean? Accidents *happen*? They occur by chance? Like an arm that hits your elbow? Or they occur inevitably because of something else?

Accidents happen. Yes. They *happen*.

I raise my hand, and the officer points at me. I stand and ask, "How much is the fine for not having a Protector?"

"You have four weeks to buy or rent," the officer answers. "Plenty of time. The deadline is easy to remember. It's parade day."

Students cheer again, and I sit down. I'm so stupid. Why did I say anything?

The officer keeps her eyes on me. "You look confused. Another question?"

"No." I shake my head. How can I explain that there must be some mix-up? Girls who read old novels and walk in the zoo and write in journals and haven't even been kissed cannot be expected to have or use a Protector.

A boy next to the aisle stands up. It's the boy who whispered complaints in the principal's office this morning. "You didn't answer the question," he shouts.

My heart races, and at first I don't understand why. Then I realize. I'm terrified for him. "She meant the *permit*," he continues. "No one can afford the permit for not having a Protector. It's a joke."

Now I'm terrified for me. I wipe my palms on my skirt and look at my feet and pray I won't have to explain my question.

The officer is calm and cool. "I'd say that no one can afford to be without a Protector. Right, students?"

Cheers erupt, and someone in the back starts a chant.

"Pro-tec-tors! Pro-tec-tors!" It's the sound of a crowd urging on their favorite team. The girl next to me is as loud as the others. Two men escort the boy out the door. No one seems to notice or care. My head pounds and the room tilts out of focus.

"Don't you dare get sick here," the girl with red hair says. "You can leave in a minute after the sponsor prizes. Just put your head down."

The safety officer bangs her Protector handle on the podium, and order returns. I close my eyes to stop the spinning room. "Buy Now has generously donated gift certificates to all new

Developers," the officer continues. "You will find credits in your school accounts."

The students clap again. Eager to escape, I open my eyes and begin to stand. But the officer continues.

"I also have a surprise," she says. "One new citizen will receive a special gift."

The principal comes on stage holding a clear bowl with pieces of paper inside. The officer draws a name from it. "Carson Fork," she announces.

Everyone looks around. The principal tells her something, and she draws again. "Hannah Cossack."

How odd that someone has a name just like mine. The girl next to me hisses, "Go!"

"What?"

"Go get your stupid prize," she says loud enough for a few kids around us to hear and snicker.

"Bring your buddy, too," the officer says, looking at the girl.

I take a deep breath and will my body to follow the girl to the stage. *Just five minutes more,* I tell myself. *Five minutes more, and everything will be okay.* We get onstage, and the officer opens a small box. She takes out a shiny, black Protector and holds it up for all to see.

"Wow," the girl whispers to me. "That's a super expensive one."

The audience claps as the officer holds the Protector out to me. I don't move. I can't move.

"Don't worry," the girl whispers again. "It's free."

I feel my lungs contract. They want me to hold it?

Sweat beads on my neck and waves of hot and cold go through my body at the same time. All the noise from minutes ago has become an eerie silence. Everyone is waiting for me.

"I can't," I say.

This comes out of my mouth louder than I expect, and I glance over at the officials who escorted the boy away. My stomach churns. Why haven't I followed my dad's instructions to follow the rules? Have I put my family in danger?

The officer isn't bothered. "New citizens are often confused," she says with a smile. "You have new responsibilities. If a crime is committed against a friend, you can help."

"Me?" I say with a barely audible voice.

"Not you alone, Hannah," she says. "You and your Protector...that's a different story."

The officer smiles again and puts my clammy hand around the Protector. She adjusts my fingers, visually measures my arm, and nods. "Good fit."

I glance down at the foreign object almost weightless in my hand. Bright gold letters on the handle proclaim, *Together We Are Strong*.

The officer faces the students. "Together good citizens stop injustice. Right, students?"

The body of people morph into a single voice. "Together we are strong!" The officer turns back to me. "Don't worry," she says. "You're assigned a buddy who will help you learn about citizenship quickly."

The Protector slips from my hand, and as the girl picks it up, my breakfast lands right in the middle of her red hair.

Jenny

"Jenny, if you're late again, points will be deducted from your grades."

I hate it when my mom opens my bedroom door without asking.

I turn over and hug my pillow. I may never get up again. Humiliated in front of the whole school. I washed my hair three times, but I know it still stinks.

"I'm not getting stuck with that stupid buddy," I say.

"Don't call people stupid," my mom says. "She was just nervous. You'll live."

The Broadcaster blares from the kitchen.

I will protest the parade. Close down the Homestead or else.

My mom rushes out. Threats are not allowed on the Broadcaster. I hear her call the safety office. It'll be another one of her busy days.

I get dressed, and when I come into the kitchen, she's working on her respond-pad.

"Mom?"

"In a sec." She turns the Broadcaster volume up and syncs her respond-pad to a work database. She presses a lot of buttons until her respond-pad beeps and flashes: Signal Untraceable.

"Another hack!" She shakes her head then looks up at me. "Protesters want to stop the parade."

"You said a few people with signs are harmless."

"There seem to be a few too many, and some of them are good with tech. Some might be citizens." She sighs and puts her respond-pad in her briefcase.

"Only someone stupid wouldn't like the parade," I say. "Like that girl. I don't want a buddy anymore."

"Sometimes you have to do things you don't like, Jenny."

"Do you think I liked not being with my friends on the most important day of my life or washing my hair a zillion times or watching someone who's no one get a cool, free Protector before I get mine?"

"Do you think I like being talked to like that?"

"Sorry," I mumble. "I didn't think being a buddy would be this terrible."

"Fine," she says. "It's your choice."

I hate it when my mom says that because it always means there really is no option but the one I don't want. It's your choice if you want to eat candy and get cavities. It's your choice if you want to waste your allowance. It's your choice if you don't finish your homework. It's never really my choice.

"Why are you making me?"

"Having a buddy is a community service that comes with a scholarship," she reminds me. "I can't send you to the Academy without a scholarship." Her slow, quiet voice makes me look down at my feet. I'm the stupid one.

I hardly ever think about my dad, but when I need something expensive, I can see that it's a lot easier for a family like Jade's. I don't know where my dad is. I never met him. Well, that's not exactly true. He left when I was four years old and has never screened or sent a Find-a-Friend or joined My Avatar community. I World-People searched him once, but there were so many Jack Morgans that I didn't get very far. Maybe when I'm eighteen I'll hire someone to find him...but probably not. I don't want to hurt my mom, and I think remembering him sometimes does.

I get up and give her a hug.

Her arms are strong around me as she asks, "You do want to go to the Academy?"

I nod. I want a career just like my grandpa's and my mom's.

"Think of this as your first assignment," she says. "You're in charge. You represent the safety office."

I'm in charge. "I'll become a great cadet and win the Safety Officer of the Year award."

"That's a few years away." My mom smiles, and I know we're back to normal. I hope she wins the award this year because there's a big cash prize—enough for her to buy a house–like she's wanted for years.

"You'll win it this year, Mom."

"I need this parade to be without incidents or..." She sighs and puts her hand on her head.

"Or what?"

"It just needs to go smoothly."

"I'll help with the parade," I offer.

She smiles. "Your responsibility is to do an exceptional job with this new girl, Hannah. Make your grandpa proud."

"I'll make you proud, Mom," I say. She kisses me quick on the cheek and heads for the door.

"We can get my Protector tonight, right? Jade's coming, too."

"Invite your buddy. You can help her choose a holder."

"Ugh…Mom! What if she causes more trouble? What if…?"

"Challenge. Responsibility. Safety officer training," my mom says as she shuts the door.

Jade will understand. I push her code on the Broadcaster, and after a few beeps, she comes into focus. Jade shakes her head and wrinkles her nose. "Is the smell gone?" she asks. "That was disgusting."

"Totally. Don't remind me," I say. "Last night I…"

"Doesn't matter," she interrupts. "Look." She holds up a beautiful, shiny, chartreuse Protector. It must be some designer model. She twirls it around her finger, smiling. "Have you ever, ever seen anything so glam?"

"But, I thought we were going together?"

"Isn't it the best?" Jade continues. "Special edition. I want to see Kyle's face when he sees this."

"Kyle?" I ask.

"Kyle Foster," she says. "I'm asking him to the parade."

My eyes stare at the screen, and I see her point out the features of her Protector, and I see her mouth move, but my brain doesn't comprehend anything. I nod and smile every once in awhile. She's asking *my* Kyle to the parade? I could never ask a boy anywhere, and if Jade liked him too, I might as well forget it.

"Hello???" Jade hollers. "Did you hear what I said about the matching accessories?"

I nod and say, "Wow," and then I grab my hairbrush from the table nearby and smile and nod some more as I brush out a tangle. With the lightest tone of voice possible I say, "You like Kyle Foster?"

"Do you even know who he is?" she asks.

"Yeah." I keep the no-big-deal tone. "He's pretty cool, I guess. He's on the debate team. But he's a Decider."

"You like the babies our age?"

"No. Course not."

"Kyle and I will be on a fab float. My dad let me choose. It's a fake amusement park with ponies and a merry-go-round and, of course, a Ferris wheel. I have a double seat reserved. Cool, right? Gotta flash. My mom's getting me a purse to match the Protector."

She starts to flash off, then says, "Hope everyone doesn't call you Barf Head." She vanishes from the screen.

Barf Head? I tell myself not to pay attention to Jade; that no one will care; that it's not a big deal, but the tears flow down my cheeks anyway. Jade. She likes Kyle, and she broke her promise about shopping together and...Barf Head? I throw down the brush.

I switch the Broadcaster to music and play the Splitting Souls song that I love over and over as loud as the volume will go. I dance and sing until I'm almost hoarse, and when I catch a glimpse of myself in the mirror, my hair is a sweaty mess, and my cheeks are red. I'm a warrior—wild and fierce and powerful. I can do anything.

I pull out my buddy information pack and punch in Hannah Cossack's connect number on my respond-pad. "This is Jenny Morgan from school," I say with authority. "I need you to screen."

"Okay," she says.

I put the Broadcaster on the connect channel and enter Hannah's number. In a moment, there she is in front of me. We look at each other in silence.

I'm losing that wild, crazed, sure feeling I had when dancing.

We talk at the same time.

"I'm sorry I—"

"Homework is—"

We try again.

"The assembly was—"

"You need to—"

We stare at each other, and then Hannah blurts out, "I'm sorry about your hair."

"Never mention my hair," I say.

"I can ask the teacher to assign me to someone else."

Part of me—a huge part—sighs with relief. *Thank you, Hannah Cossack, for letting me escape and go back to things like they were before yesterday.* But I remember my mom and the Academy.

"It's community service credit," I say.

"You can do something else."

"This is what I want to do," I say, trying to convince myself.

"Why?"

Hannah's whole face seems to ask the question. Her eyes widen, and I see she has light blue eyes and dark eyelashes that stand out against her fair skin. Her long, blond hair is straight and pulled half back, half down. She knows how to style it.

I can't tell her I have no choice if I want to go to the Academy. "Be a responsible helper, and you contribute to the community," I say.

"Is that what the Broadcaster says?" she asks.

"Yes. Citizens learn lots from the Broadcaster," I say.

I check the time and think about telling her more that I've learned from the Broadcaster, but when I look back at the screen, she's looking at some weird thing in her hand and moving it around in the light. "What are you holding?" I ask.

She lifts what looks like some funny monkeys all attached together. They're sitting side by side with their legs crossed. The first one has its hands over its eyes, like a blindfold. The second one has its hands over its ears like it's blocking out a loud noise, and the third has its hands over its mouth. The whole thing is purple and about half the size of her hand.

"Dolls? How old are you?"

"Almost sixteen, and it's not a doll. It's a figurine of three wise monkeys: Mizaru, Kikazaru, and Iwazaru. I collect them."

Maybe she's from some strange country I haven't heard of. "Is that your language?"

She laughs a little like I've made a joke. It's not a mean laugh like Jade has sometimes, more like a laugh from someone older when a little kid does something kind of cute but silly.

"It's Japanese. See no evil. Hear no evil. Speak no evil." She says this like she's teaching me something important.

But I remember that I'm the one in charge. "That's totally dumb, and if it's religious or something, you can't pass it around in school."

"It's just an old saying," she sighs. "Some people think there should be four monkeys."

Three monkeys, four monkeys, a hundred monkeys. Why would I care?

"Do you like real monkeys?" she asks. "I think they're fun to watch."

With 3500 Broadcaster channels and video games and music muffs and respond-pad reach-outs, why would anyone watch a bunch of caged monkeys?

I notice the time. If I don't leave in one minute, I'll be late. It would be the third time this month, and they'll call my mom.

"Monkeys are stupid, and they stink," I answer. "I have to leave for school. Do you have any questions?" I don't wait for a response. There's no time for foolish conversation. "Mr. Thomas only checks English homework on Wednesdays because he has a night job. Make sure you have the fastest internet connection, or your online work takes the whole afternoon. Get your gym uniform at Buy Now unless you want the colors all weird. And remember the parade. Watch for the notice on your respond-pad."

"What do you mean?"

"You'll be on the float. It's your reward for passing citizenship orientation."

I smile, thinking about the parade. At least I'll be on a float, even if it's not sitting beside Kyle on a Ferris wheel. "Can't you just picture it? You'll be high up like a celebrity, and wave to everyone in the street."

"I don't want to be on the float."

How can this girl be so dense?

"You won't be by yourself," I say. "Buddies ride together."

"I don't want to be on the float."

My stomach churns. I'm tired of people who ruin things for others. No more being nice. Forget the shopping trip; I'll tell my mom she's sick.

"You're a citizen now," I say and look straight into her eyes. "Citizens love the parade, and riding on the float is a rule. You carry your Protector everywhere and use it according to the rules. I'll be checking. It's part of my job. Do you have any more questions?"

She shakes her head and squeezes the monkey thing. "I didn't make the law."

I narrow my eyes and take a step closer to the Broadcaster. "All that matters is that you follow it."

And then I black out the screen.

Hannah

I've spent a week at the new school.

I do my homework every night (in ten minutes).

I do not ask questions.

I am the perfect citizen.

Last night, at dinner, my parents asked how many friends I have made. I'm waiting for them to suggest I hang a sign around my neck that says, *I'm Hannah. Now available for new friendship.* Cliques are already full–especially for opportunity people. Some opportunity kids try to impress by flashing new Protectors and pretending to be lifelong citizens. They get invited to lunch tables.

But, it's Monday. A new week. I'll try. The boy who made all the negative Governcorp comments on the first day is in my English class. His name is Rad. He doesn't say much, but I assume we have things in common.

"I was worried you were in trouble after asking the Protector question," I tell him before class.

"We've still got *some* rights."

I nod. Sounds like what Kyle says.

"Doesn't hurt that my cousin's a lawyer," he adds without smiling.

My respond-pad flashes a reminder message about the parade. I angle it so Rad can read it too.

He smirks. "Yeah, right."

"You're not going?"

"I'll be there. Believe me, I'll be there."

The teacher enters, and Rad moves away. When class is over, he leaves before I can ask any more questions.

I stop at my locker and find Jenny and another girl in front of it.

"Excuse me," I say to the girl who blocks my way. She has "Fashion Slave" written all over her.

"Oh, it's Buddy," she laughs.

I refuse to react.

"Buddy is such a cute name for a dog."

"My locker," I say.

"Oh, it talks. Can it roll over, too?"

"Stop, Jade, or I'll get in trouble," Jenny says.

Thanks for the help, I think.

Jade moves just enough for me to open my locker door. "One day, Jenny, you could be in charge of watching all of Middletown, and I'll be a top Governcorp official," Jade says. "We'll work together to get rid of the horrible Homestead."

"I don't think the buildings are that terrible," Jenny says.

"I'm not talking about the buildings," Jade says as she stares at me.

I find my things as fast I can, but not fast enough. Three more of Jade's fashion shadows crowd around me.

"They should come up with a different name," someone says. "Buddy sounds too friendly."

"Here, Buddy. Here, Buddy," Jade calls. "I want to see some tricks."

Where are the viewers when you need them? I wonder. I keep my hands on my backpack. It's heavy enough to do some damage. The jokes keep coming as the girls block my path. My heart races as they crowd shoulder-to-shoulder and I feel the cold metal handle of the locker press against my back. I feel sweat growing on my brow as I remember they all have Protectors.

"Maybe they should be on leashes," says a girl with a crooked nose.

"They could be taught to fetch whatever we want," says someone else.

"They could have their own separate doggie doors when they go in and out of buildings," Jade adds.

Jenny laughs as loud as the others and says, "Instead of face powder, we'll get them flea powder."

I have to keep my head. I lean toward the nearest girl. "Watch out," I say. "I just ate."

"Ugh!" She jumps back.

"Gross," someone else says as they give me some space.

The viewer speaker in the hall comes on at last: "Girls in the Developer locker area, get to class. Get to class now."

"Thanks for getting us in trouble, Jenny," Jade snaps as she leads the others down the hall. I wait for Jenny to protest the accusation but instead, she glares at me. I stare right back until she scrambles down the hall after the group.

After school, I walk home alone and try to calculate how many days until my best friend, Maria, will be a citizen. Five months? A year? She said her family was saving every spare token, and if they owed nine hundred tokens two weeks ago, and they save less than a hundred each month? That's too many months to wait.

I watch someone crisscross the street a block ahead. It's Kyle. He crosses again. He has to be the least viewed citizen in the country. He has maps showing all the viewer locations. He sits down next to someone under a tree.

I run to catch up with him, and as I get closer, I see the other person is Jonah. He used to live in the Homestead, too. I think about turning around, but Kyle stands up and waves at me. I walk over. Jonah concentrates on his respond-pad and doesn't look up. Kyle gently pulls me down into a spot between them—a little too close to Jonah. I wiggle toward Kyle, and he says, "The viewers can't see here."

Jonah shifts positions and lies on his side to stretch his long legs. He punches away at the respond-pad, his beret tilting over one eye. A beret? Why does Kyle associate with him? It's not that I don't like Jonah—I never spent time with him—it's just that he has a reputation. He's over eighteen, out of school, and if rumors are even somewhat accurate, in trouble most of the time. I've heard he's a thief. People say he steals things from Governcorp, and I know he's stolen hearts. Several girls in the Homestead had crushes on him before he gained citizenship a year ago. His dark hair is thick, and there's something about his deep-set eyes that make him seem invincible. His skin is the perfect color of bronze. I can't help but notice the muscles under his black pullover shirt. I take a second glance at it. I think it's just like the one I saw Rad wear the first day of school.

Jonah looks at me and follows my gaze down to his shirt. "You like it?" he asks. I could kill myself for falling into his trap.

"It's a weird black shirt. What's to like?" I shift positions and pretend to have a leg cramp and move away.

"See, Kyle?" Jonah says.

"I still don't think you should wear it," Kyle argues.

Jonah shrugs and returns to his respond-pad.

I steal another look at the shirt. There are white circles and lines and squiggles from the center down. It's the same shirt. What does it mean?

"You doing okay?" Kyle asks me.

"Sure." I fake a smile.

"Don't eat before the next assembly," Jonah pipes in. He doesn't bother to look up, but I see the smirk.

"Kyle?!"

"It's no big deal," Kyle answers. "If someone forced a Protector into my hand, I'd puke too."

"Nothing wrong with being a troublemaker," Jonah says.

I deliberately ignore him and turn to Kyle. "Where's your Protector?"

Before Kyle can answer, Jonah pulls my new Protector from my backpack.

"Put it back. I don't want to look at it," I insist.

"New model," he says to Kyle.

I feel my stomach rumbling. "Put it back," I say with conviction.

Jonah examines it inch by inch but manages to watch me the whole time too. At last, he returns it to the backpack. I feel myself exhale.

"Where's yours?" This time I direct the question to Jonah.

He smiles and goes back to his respond-pad. "Out for repairs," he says without looking up. "Right, Kyle?"

"Some of us…me…others…" Kyle fumbles for words as he pulls out his wallet. He gives me a card. It's a permit that says he is allowed to be without a Protector.

"I thought the permit was expensive. Where did you get enough money?" I ask.

"Yeah…well…there are ways," Jonah says.

"Kyle?"

"Come to the meeting," Kyle says. "Join our group, Citizens for True Democracy."

"Join an anti-Governcorp group two weeks after my dad earned us citizenship? I don't have to tell you how hard he worked–he slaved–for ten years."

"That's the point," Kyle says. "No one should have to do that. Come to the meeting, and I'll work on a permit for you."

"An illegal permit," I say as I glance at Jonah.

"Lots of people agree with us," Kyle continues. He pulls out a form from his backpack and shows it to me. "We're organizing a peaceful demonstration at the parade."

"A way to get people in trouble."

"Peaceful." He makes me laugh by putting the palms of his hands together and bowing like a Yogi. "Sooooo peaceful."

"Good to go," Jonah says as he strikes a key on his respond-pad. Kyle seems to know what he means, and I don't ask.

"The protest is perfectly legal," Kyle continues. He holds up some forms. "I could use your help to distribute these to new Developers." Before I can respond, the nearby Broadcaster blares out a Governcorp announcement:

Official report: Twelve-year-old honored for protecting grandmother in house burglary attempt.

Citizen announcements follow, and I start to talk.

"Hold on," Jonah interrupts. He wants to hear the Broadcaster noise?

Send us the news. Sunshine at dawn. Citizens unite against the laws. Apply for a permit to protest at the parade.

Jonah glances at Kyle, and they give each other a thumbs-up. That announcement about the protest must be what he programmed into the Broadcaster system. I'm sure it's illegal.

"We'll have hundreds of citizens and opportunity people who want reform at the parade," Kyle says with wide eyes. "We believe peaceful and decent is the way to change people's minds about Protectors – change minds about all the laws. We don't use Protectors because we want to get rid of them." His earnest eyes light up with each word, but he hasn't seen the change in people who live in the Homestead. Most seem to want the privilege of Protectors as soon as they walk out the gates. They feel they've earned it by hard labor and sacrifice. Using a Protector–especially against an opportunity person–even brings instant status as a new citizen; "You're one of us now."

"Do you remember Max from building five?" I ask Kyle. "He used his Protector against someone he knew for years, just to act like a good citizen."

"He's just one person."

"Did you see all the students cheer for Protectors at the assembly?" I ask.

"I didn't cheer," Kyle says. "Did you?"

"Of course not," I say.

"We have to speak up about what the Homesteads are like. What Opportunity people go through."

"No one cares, Kyle," I argue.

"How 'bout you? Do you care if some Opportunity person dies for no reason?" His look is piercing, and his voice is so reproachful that tears come to my eyes.

"That's unfair," I say. But what he says is true. People from the Homestead are often attacked and even killed for minor or ridiculous reasons, and Governcorp always supports the citizens involved.

"Citizens don't care that good people are treated like crap and expected to do menial jobs for years," Kyle continues. "Every year it's harder to become a citizen."

"Take it down a notch, Caesar," Jonah says. "She doesn't have her armor today."

I swallow down tears as I get up and walk away.

"Hannah, I'm sorry," Kyle says. "I get…"

"Yeah, he gets that way," Jonah interrupts.

"I just want to make things better," Kyle says pumping his fist.

"This isn't just about me," I say. "I can't pass out flyers or protest or do anything that Governcorp would consider against the law because that would put my family at risk for deportation. I need to do the right thing."

Jonah stands and fixes his beret. "So, do the right thing," he says to me with his half smile. "I'd say you're a natural."

I'm not sure if I'm uneasy because he thinks I'm a rebel or because his eyes are glued to mine. He raises his eyebrows at me, and I want to say, "You're a jerk," but I decide to cut him some slack. Besides, calling someone like Jonah a jerk would be an encouragement.

"Broadcaster announcements will come through pretty steady," he says to Kyle. "Mixed up the signals. They won't be traced."

I think about asking questions about his protest announcements, but I don't want Jonah to think I'm interested in anything he does. I'm not. At least that's what I tell myself.

"Keep your head on straight," Jonah says to Kyle. He turns to go, and like magic, I see them. Monkeys. The design on the bottom of Jonah's shirt is drawn in such a way that you need to be at just the correct angle to view them. It's like those books of optical illusions or 3D pictures that your eyes have to adjust to. If you're not looking at it the right way, the images don't exist.

Jonah whistles as he walks across the street. Okay, I watch. It's not a crime. I don't know what he does or why he wears berets and has on a looped-out shirt. But right now, I don't care. Thoughts race through my head and make my pulse pound. He's mysterious, stupid, dangerous, bad news...and wow...crazy-hot good-looking.

Kyle clears his throat. "I'd say forget him, but he's okay."

"What?" I say as I feel my cheeks warm. "I have to get home."

"Just think about joining us," he says. I shake my head. "At least take some forms to leave around the school." He puts some in my backpack. I don't protest. I can throw them away later.

"It's perfectly legal," he says again.

His passion makes me smile. "When you're a lawyer, you can change everything," I say.

But Kyle's face is solemn, and I feel goose bumps on my arms when he says, "It might be too late by then."

Jenny

Eighty-six screens cover the walls of the safety office. They slowly rotate live feeds from 5,679 viewers in the city. My mom's in charge of it all. I see people pass buildings, eat in the park, walk dogs, and shop. I type *All Clear* into the report panel.

I come to the safety office after school almost every day. A year ago, I begged my mom's assistant, Carmichael, to let me watch him operate everything. Then I begged him to let me sit at the controls. I imitated everything he did, and now I can do the job as well as he can. He lets me do the work while he reads comics or plays cards or takes a long lunch. My mom doesn't like it that he's so lazy, but her boss is Carmichael's uncle, so she doesn't say much. I punch in South Street on the control panel to watch Jade and our group walk home. I'd wave, but I know they can't see me. I glance at Carmichael on the other side of the room. He's still busy with a comic book and chips. I slide on the headphones and open the security listener. I can pretend it's official business, can't I?

Jade comes in loud and clear. "I can't believe she didn't follow the rules. You know what will happen, right?" Everyone laughs and then they walk out of range. The laughing reminds me of what happened at the lockers with Hannah. When lots of people are laughing at the same time, it makes you laugh too. You may not even think anything is funny. It's…contagious. Like catching a germ. It's not your fault. I pull up the next screen.

"So, my plan is to—" Jade is saying. Carmichael pulls the headphones off my ears before Jade finishes the sentence.

"You're killin' me," he says. "Stay out of trouble for five minutes and come watch my card trick."

I put away the headphones and walk over to his side of the room.

"Why do you like cards so much?" I ask.

"Prize money," he says as he pulls a card from behind my ear. "Best trick this year gets five thousand tokens."

Governcorp sponsors different contests every year during parade week to celebrate the laws.

"Check this out." Carmichael fans the cards in his hand. He puts down a queen, a king, a jack, and an ace. "Four Good Citizens," he says. "The Queen collects the immigrant children." Carmichael shuffles, and all the small cards show up under the Queen. "Those are the kids. See?"

"Because they're small numbers?" I ask.

"Right," he nods.

"Next, Kings make the laws, and Aces give money to the Kings they like. Everyone promises to help the Jacks," he explains as he shuffles again.

An ace, a king, and a jack of spades show up. Then an ace, a king, and a jack of clubs.

"I don't get it, but it's pretty cool." I laugh and grab his Protector and pretend to shoot each pile.

"What is wrong with you?" My mom's booming voice makes me jump, and I drop the Protector. "We can't ID people if the tracers aren't working," she says to Carmichael. "I told you to work on them."

"Sorry," Carmichael answers as he picks up the Protector. "I was—"

"Busy?" my mom says. "It's a team effort, Carmichael. And I'm sure you have homework, Jenny."

Carmichael shoves his cards in a drawer, and I move to the desk where I do my homework. I pull out my respond-pad but I pay more attention to my mom than math. She projects a map on the wall. It's the parade route. "We'll block off South Street and keep all protesters west of here," she says. "Barricades, extra viewers, and Broadcasters over here by the Grandstand. The Comfort Center will triple their staff on the ground and have choppers in the air ready to pick up troublemakers. Got that?"

Carmichael nods.

"Good," my mom says. "Any more problem reports?"

"I counted eighteen," Carmichael says. "Store owner, restaurant hostess, cab driver...bunch of randos. How do you live with yourself when you see a crime committed and do nothing?"

"If I had *my* protector, I'd use it," I pipe in. My mom couldn't take me shopping last night because of work–*again.*

She ignores me and keeps talking to Carmichael. "Get evidence."

"They avoided the viewers somehow," he says. "One person's word against another."

"We need this under control," my mom says. "We have never had so many citizens do this, and it has to be stopped before—" She doesn't finish her sentence because her Governcorp beeper goes off. Instead, she says, "Jenny, will you make some coffee?"

I know she's trying to get rid of me, but I don't mind because I don't like to watch her talk to Vince Flakeman. I know she disagrees with him a lot and wants to tell him where to go, but instead, she swallows hard and just says, "Yes, sir."

As I go into the break room, she calls after me, "I promise to shop tonight."

"Yes!" I say to myself, and give a sigh of relief as I measure the coffee. My mom's loud voice makes me curious, and I open the door a crack so I can listen.

"I realize there have been incidents lately," she says. "If I had money for another equipment technician? Of course. Shareholder profits."

She doesn't say anything for a few seconds, and I think the conversation is over until I hear her say, "I understand the warning. There won't be any mistakes."

She hangs up, and I'm about to come out when I hear Carmichael say, "My uncle is such an asshole sometimes. He wouldn't fire you unless…you know; just keep costs down and people quiet. Main part of the job, right?"

Fire my mom? She is the best safety officer there is. Keep costs down for Governcorp? But we're the ones who need extra money. Officers don't earn high salaries. How will we ever get a house?

"Jenny," my mom calls. "Is that coffee ready?"

I bring it out ready to tell my mom she's doing a great job, but she's already too busy to listen to me. She points out viewers to Carmichael. "See?" she says. "Three eighty-nine; sixty-two; and thirteen fifty-four are down. The viewers have to ID troublemakers in key areas for us to keep order."

She hands Carmichael a list of repairs. "Get them operational."

"Stop wasting my time!" I jump as the loud voice comes from inside the door. My mom and Carmichael have their Protectors in position faster than I can turn around. "Put those down and don't leave the door open if you don't like visitors," the woman adds. She's waving a safety office form.

My mom scowls at Carmichael. I feel bad for him under her glare, but he needs to be more careful; he always forgets to reset the door code. He mumbles, "Sorry," and leaves.

Now I recognize the woman–Susan Frey. She and my mom were friends in law school. She came to our house when I was little, but I haven't seen her in forever.

"Hi, Susan," I say and smile wide.

She squints at me. "Is it really you? That preschooler who taught me how to color?" She gives me a hug. My mom clears her throat, but I hug Susan back.

"You're all grown up," she says.

"Just in the Developing level at school," I say.

"And that hair!" She touches my curls and gives me a huge smile. "I bet you're fighting off the boys."

I shake my head and blush.

"Jenny," my mom interrupts. "Your homework."

Before I even sit down to work, my mom and Susan begin to argue.

"You can't restrict protester permits," Susan says.

"You're holding the form that says I can, and I did," my mom snaps. "Fifty lucky people will be on the other side of town. Everyone on both sides can have a good time and then go home."

They keep arguing about protesters, so I go back into the break room, where a Broadcaster blares to an empty room:

Tree pollen sucks. Ripe fruit will rot if you forget it. The Homestead has excellent doctors and teachers. Four monkeys escaped their zoo cages. What's not to like? Send us the news.

I wonder how the monkeys escaped? My respond-pad beeps a message. Fashion Club reminder. I'll see Jade at the meeting and show off my Protector. I wonder why my mom doesn't like Susan anymore? I think best friends should be forever. Another beep. Buddy meeting? Two weeks of torture to go before I can get back to normal.

Hannah

Friday–end of week two.

I go to classes.

I do not ask questions.

I am the perfect citizen.

In math, I offer to explain to the girl next to me what the teacher apparently can't, and I'm reminded to please be quiet.

In science, a second-year Decider shows me his black-and-purple Protector. He says he used it once in a restaurant when a guy was sneaking out without paying. He wants to see my new model. I refuse to bring it out. He says I'm weird and need to be rewired. He looks for another lab partner.

In English, I want to talk to Rad again, but this is the third day in a row he hasn't shown up. The teacher says Rad may miss the rest of the semester for an illness.

In Study Hall, my lab notebook for science class is missing. I see Mr. Black-and-Purple Protector at a nearby table. "Beats me," he says when I ask him about it. "Check lost and found." Everyone at the table roars with laughter.

I go to the office. The school viewer officer leads me to several huge boxes in a corner. She glances at my worn shirt. "Today's lost-and-found dump day, so it's okay to help yourself."

"I'm looking for a lab notebook."

"Oh?" she smirks. "We don't get many books in lost and found, but help yourself."

A viewer buzzer calls her back to her post, and I'm relieved she won't be able to watch me. She's right about the books. I find one old textbook and the rest are clothes and T-shirts for weird wail-bands like Strep Throat and Contamination, which I throw on the floor. At the bottom of the last box, I find the lab notebook, ruined with marker and scissors. I toss it. As I put the clothes back, I catch a glimpse of a familiar black shirt with a white design at the bottom. I pull it out and tell myself I think the design is cool and that's the only reason I want to have it. I glance at the officer. She's busy with the viewer, so I slip the shirt into my backpack. I don't want to give her the satisfaction of knowing I took something, but as I leave, I feel her smirk follow me out the door.

Are there still just twenty-four hours in a day?

I wait for Jenny at her locker since my respond-pad notified me of a mandatory buddy meeting.

The ever-popular Jade greets me. "Learn any new tricks to-day?" she says.

"I did notice a disgusting smell," I say. "Seems to be coming from your direction."

"Don't push me, alien," she barks.

"Sorry I'm late," Jenny says as she comes around the corner.

Jade and I answer at the same time.

"It's annoying."

"That's okay."

Jenny frowns and looks my way. "I was talking to Jade," she says. "Did you want something?"

"We have a meeting." I hold up my respond-pad notice.

"Ugh! Forgot."

"Thanks, Jenny, for making me stand here for no reason," Jade says as she walks away. "Have fun with dog training…and your math homework."

"Jade!" Jenny whines after her. "I'll only be a sec. I have my Splitting Soul Protector to show you."

"You know the fashion club's rules." Jade's expression is smug. "No one can come late. And everyone's over Splitting Souls." She enters the room for the meeting and closes the door with a bang.

I glance over at Jenny. I don't say anything, but my expression must show my loathing.

"She just likes to joke," Jenny says without even a twinge of a smile. "Best friends joke with each other."

I turn away and wonder how long a person can ignore reality. Best friend?

Buddy Meeting.

I hope it's the last torture of the day.

We head to the classroom, and the woman in charge shows us how to send a message to the Broadcaster–a citizen privilege. It takes two minutes to learn, but she teaches it again and again.

"All information is welcome on the Broadcaster," she says with her broad smile. "Your news. Your way." She repeats this every time a student sends a practice message.

Jenny looks at me and rolls her eyes. We both smile.

At the break, Jenny pulls me aside. "Let's go," she says.

"Can we? Isn't it a rule violation?" I ask.

"I'm feeling sick," she says. "Aren't you?"

Jenny

I thought I'd croak if I had to stay in that meeting one more second. Did that teacher think everyone was that dumb? I race to fashion club and open the door; everyone is gone. I let out a groan.

Hannah sees the empty room too. "Sorry," she says.

I can tell she means it, but that doesn't help my friendship with Jade or solve my math problems. I picture myself in my safety officer uniform. I stand up straight and give myself a pep talk. "I will complete my assignment and continue this community service credit as promised."

"What?"

"I will complete my assignment and—"

"You're imitating Officer Robot," Hannah says with a laugh.

"I was using an official, professional voice, and besides, I don't watch that show anymore," I say.

Hannah tilts her head to the side, fakes a smile, then jerks her arms up and down like the television cartoon, Officer Robot. "I will complete this assignment and continue my community service credit." She sounds just like him. She lowers her arms. "It's a good show," she says.

"For little kids."

Hannah shrugs like it's not a big deal if I still watch it. (I sometimes do.) "I watch it with my sisters," she says.

We walk out the door and turn in the same direction. Before I can decide to walk in front of her or in back or go faster or stop, Hannah pulls something out of her pocket.

"Want to see?" She holds out a blue, marble monkey thing.

"I would never waste my time with monkey dolls," I say.

"I told you before–they're called figurines."

She's using a teacher voice again, and I want to tell her to stop, but she keeps going.

"Monkeys like to imitate, too. It makes them feel safe to know they're all acting the same way. And if a person tries to copy them, they play along and copy back. They don't understand what they're doing."

"Four of them were stupid and ran away from the zoo," I say. Why did I blurt that out? I don't care about the stupid monkeys. Why am I even talking to this girl?

"Would you like to be confined in a small space?" Hannah says. "I think they left their cages because they're smart and brave."

"I don't think monkeys can be smart or brave. Did you do your math?"

"What?" she says.

"It's an official question. I'm supposed to check and help with any problem assignments."

"I had no problem, Mr. Official." She laughs and salutes like Officer Robot, and I can't help but smile. Still, her answer can't be right.

I fold my arms and face her. "You got number four?"

She shrugs. "Yeah."

I frown and stare at her a second, but she's more concerned with wiping some dirt off her monkey thing. She glances up. "My mom is a teacher. I can explain the problem to you."

I take a step back and raise my chin. "It was the easiest math home-work ever. But I need you to send it to me as an official assignment."

"Whatever you say," Hannah smirks and walks away.

I can feel my cheeks getting red. Why did I start this conversa-tion in the first place? "I send in reports," I say.

"What reports?"

"Your progress." I stop and read from my respond-pad. "You enjoy your new environment, you follow the news on the Broad-caster, and complete your homework."

"You don't know if I do any of those things," Hannah says.

"I just give the right answers, that's what matters." Does she think I would bother to find out things about her?

The Broadcaster nearby reminds listeners of the parade and some other stuff about Homestead doctors and schools.

"Do you ever listen to the Broadcaster?" Hannah asks.

She must be crazy. How could I not listen? The Broadcasters are everywhere. "I don't have a hearing disability," I say.

"It says Homestead schools are good. But why do kids have to go back two grades to catch up when they become citizens?"

"They didn't study or do their homework." *Easy answer,* I think.

"It says Homestead doctors are good. But why do Opportunity kids get sick all the time? Why do they need shots when they go to a citizen school?"

"They skip their checkups," I say. *Why is she asking so many questions?*

"The Broadcaster never says that people are hungry in the Homestead. Sometimes people our age steal food for their families."

"The Broadcaster tells us everything important," I say.

"It twists facts. Listen to it carefully sometime, and you'll see."

I would never admit to her that I do hear hard-to-believe things on the Broadcaster. But I wouldn't call them wrong–more like jokes.

"Look," I say. "I'm sure you want to be with your friends and not waste time going to buddy meetings, so I'll just keep sending things in and saying one of us is sick or busy with a school project or something, and then we don't have to go anymore. Okay?"

Hannah doesn't say anything, but what is there to complain about?

I can't tell if we're still going in the same direction, so I decide to run ahead. I yell back, "Take your Protector everywhere. I get extra points 'cause you have yours before the deadline. See you on the parade float."

Hannah

Iwatch Jenny run off and look up to see a not-so-well-hidden viewer. I shouldn't have told her those truths about the Home-stead. Speaking out against policies is a sure way to be deported or…sent to the Comfort Center for rehabilitation. Just the thought of what can happen there makes my heart pound. A person never comes out the same. I saw it in neighbors back at the Homestead. Mr. Wright can only talk gibberish. Juan Morez lost his memory. Mrs. Koboyashi just never came back at all. I shake away these thoughts. Jenny is right about one thing. I need my friends.

I walk to the Homestead, and as it comes into view, I think of the old saying, "Looks are deceiving." Who would guess that inside this beautiful square mile compound are places barely inhabitable? The grass is green, and plots of every type of flower are professionally cared for all year long. The garbage and recycling bins are neatly stacked, and the streets are clean. The ten-story brick buildings are sturdy, and the trees tall. There is a park with swings and benches near the winding paths.

"It's so beautiful," citizens say. "Opportunity families are so fortunate to have what Governcorp provides." Very few born citizens ever enter the gates, except for building dedications when Governcorp gives prizes for citizens to tour a new facility. Citizens don't know and probably wouldn't care that the new stoves and washers and beds on display are given to Governcorp employees soon after the dedication. Opportunity people never get new things. Some adults swear they will try to get Governcorp to change once they become citizens, but no one takes the risk. They're already free. Who would jeopardize that?

"Soon you'll be a citizen too," I remember my dad telling Maria's father as we left. My dad will never go back. Friendships end. The have's and have-nots. I've seen both sides break it off. I'll never let that happen with Maria.

At the east gate, I hesitate when I see the ID machine. Governcorp is proud of its detailed records. If my dad finds out, he will not approve that I came back to visit so soon. Governcorp will think you're not adjusting well to citizenship, he'll say. I shove in my ID and open the gate. Governcorp officials think what they want anyway.

I walk through the large square and past my old school. Just like with housing, at the school's dedication, citizens saw a wonderful place: the desks shiny, new respond-pads in all the classrooms; young, bright teachers. The next week when classes started, the furnishings had been replaced by junk and the teachers were replaced by citizens with no credentials.

I walk to Building C and go inside. The smell from gas and sewer leaks takes my breath away, and I cough and gasp. I've already gotten used to clean air. The inside looks just the same as it had when we lived here. The hall carpet is worn bare in the middle, and the cement block walls have a grayish hue from smoke, dirt, and neglect. Paint peels from the ceiling and bare light bulbs flicker from bad wiring.

I walk the seven flights of stairs rather than chance the elevator. By the time I get to the door, I'm sweating and my head pounds from the lack of ventilation. I pause to catch my breath at the door that had been my home. No, I don't wish I still lived in this stifling place. But breathing clean air isn't the same as feeling free. I pass the old kitchen that everyone on the floor uses and turn the corner by the communal bathroom.

"They can't do it. They can't!" A teenage girl bolts out the bathroom door and slams into me. It's Zora. Her sobbing mother comes out after her. Zora doesn't bother to apologize to me but turns to her mother and continues. "I'm not leaving. There are protest groups to join. There are fighters."

"Do you want to be killed?" her mom asks.

"They treat us like animals. I feel dead already."

Mrs. Malta looks at me and wipes away a few tears. "The notice came this morning," she says. "It's been ten years."

I look at Zora's face, full of fear as much as anger. If a family hasn't paid its citizenship taxes in ten years, they lose their Homestead apartment and are deported. They have no choice about where they are sent. Countries are always looking for slave labor.

"You." Zora points her long, gold-painted fingernail at me like a weapon. "You're out," she says. I guess she means out of the Homestead. She glares at me and steps closer. "Did you cheat? Pay bribes?"

"No," I say.

"How'd your parents get Governcorp jobs?" It's an accusation, not a question.

I think about how my dad collapsed every night after standing and lifting boxes for ten hours at the grocery store, and how my mom taught all day and then worked nights and holidays as a tutor for Governcorp kids instead of having some time to herself. When my dad became a citizen, he was allowed to manage the store. And my mom found a citizen's teaching job thanks to a parent of a child she'd tutored.

"Hannah's parents are honest," Mrs. Malta says. "They were lucky."

My parents—our family—is lucky. All the Homestead adults work just as hard as my parents did, and many teenagers stop school and get menial jobs to help earn enough money in time. Mrs. Malta works in a Homestead factory that makes viewers, and on weekends she and Zora do face painting and fortune telling at birthday parties for citizen children. Nothing pays much. I wish I could think of something hopeful to say.

"I'm not squirming for Governcorp," Zora sneers at me. "They lowered wages and raised taxes again. This time we'll protest."

I can't imagine Zora peacefully protesting anything. Can she be part of Kyle's group?

"Get out of my hallway, Citizen," Zora says with no effort to hide the contempt on her face. "Get out before I grab your Protector and use it on you."

A chill goes up my spine before Mrs. Malta takes her arm and leads her away. Without warning, Zora turns and throws her whole body at me, and I crash into the wall so hard I lose my breath. She grabs my backpack and turns it upside down.

"Stop!" Mrs. Malta hollers as my things fly everywhere. I fight for the backpack, but Zora is stronger and pushes me away again. My body muscles tighten, and when the Protector falls out, I lunge for it. Zora tries to grab it too, but I'm quicker this time. I point it right at her head.

"What are you doing?" Maria comes out of her apartment and into the hall.

My jaw is set, and my hand is snug around the Protector.

"What are you doing!?" Maria shouts this time.

I blink and look at Maria, then Zora, then the Protector. My arm falls to my side, the Protector still inexplicably glued to my hand.

Mrs. Malta puts her arm around Zora and ushers her back to their apartment. My heart races and my breaths burst in and out like I've run a marathon.

Maria stiffens and takes a step back. "You *got* one?" she says.

"It's not like that," I try to explain. The cold feel of the Protector suddenly repulses me, and I throw it in the backpack, pick up the stuff in the hall, and bury it again.

"Were you going to shoot her?"

"No." My legs are so shaky I'm not sure they can hold my weight. I lean against the wall to stay standing.

Maria walks away.

I feel tears swell. "Maria, please," I say. "I hate everything just like you do. I hate my school. I have no friends. I hate being a citizen."

I've been thinking this so long, but I surprise myself when I say it. A viewer in the corner catches my eye. What have I done? What if someone is watching right now?

"It's broken," Maria says as she tosses her long, black braid behind her back. "Come out of the hall."

She gives me lemonade, and we sit in silence for a long time. Then I tell her about the school and all the horrible students and the assembly and how I got the Protector and Jenny.

"All over her hair?" she asks.

We both laugh, and I can tell she's forgiven me, and we begin to talk like old friends again.

I tell her about my sisters' infatuation with sofa beds, and she tells me about her brother's baseball team, and we look at fashions we can't afford on my respond-pad. We gossip about people we know and argue about which new band is in and which movie star will get married or divorced. All the while, my mind whirls with what happened with Zora. What if Maria hadn't come out in the hallway…? So, this is how it happens. A moment of fear or anger or insanity; built up tension from previous encounters. A turning point that can't be explained in facts; just emotion. A second that changes everything.

"Hello?" Maria nudges me out of my thoughts.

"Do you think opportunity people will protest like Zora said?" I ask.

"How's your school cafeteria?"

"It's horrible. Don't change the subject."

"What subject?"

"Kyle said there was a meeting soon. What's it about?"

"Have no idea."

"You're a bad liar."

"I don't know details, okay?" Maria picks up a shoe and tosses it in the closet. "But, maybe protesting could be a good thing."

"My dad says complaining just makes Governcorp raise taxes and turn off services. How can causing trouble help?" I ask.

"I'm not saying fight like Zora…but doing nothing just seems…"

"Follow the rules, and you will get out of here," I say. "We'll be together all the time again and figure things out." I don't like to plead, but I can tell she's not convinced. "Please," I say. "Be safe." She nods, and we hug each other goodbye as the Broadcaster in her living room blares.

Keep shoelaces tied or you'll trip. Homestead schools teach our national values. Sunshine at dawn. Everyone loves the parade.

We look at each other and mimic the Broadcaster sign-off together. "What's not to like?" At least we can still laugh.

My chest feels heavy as I approach the exit to the Homestead. I hate to leave Maria. I pull out my ID and realize my hands are shaking. It takes two tries to get my ID card in the machine. I make myself breathe. When I finally exit the gate, my whole body is shaking. I pulled out the Protector. Like all the citizens I loathe, I pulled out the Protector. Why? Because I had it? Because as a citizen, I can use it anytime against opportunity people? My throat tightens, and my stomach churns. I won't let this new life and Governcorp make me into someone I hate. But if I did it once, does that mean…? I'll leave the Protector at home until I figure out a way to never carry it again.

Jenny

The hall is almost clear of students as I search inside my locker for junk food. If I don't get a sugar rush soon, my brain is going to explode! I'm late for math, which I wouldn't care about, except this is the review day, and I still don't understand anything about this chapter. My mom wants me in the safety office right after school, but I need to make up with Jade and copy her math answers. I have tons of homework in every subject, and that stupid Hannah hasn't sent me any of her assignments.

I grab a cookie package on the locker floor. Empty.

"Hey, Jenny," Russell says as he opens his locker.

"Hi," I mumble.

"Bad day?"

"Bad day, bad week, bad life," I moan. "Do you have any candy?"

Russell shakes his head.

"Jade would have some. But right now, my best friend hates me."

"That's an oxymoron…maybe it's a paradox."

"Sure," I nod my head. I don't want to figure out Russell right now.

He sighs. "It's okay to ask me," he says. "Aren't you ever curious about something you don't understand?"

What I'm curious about, and what I don't understand, is why Jade can't accept that I have to be a buddy and why Hannah makes it worse by being so annoying. I can't tell Russell all that. Instead, I say, "Do people ever drive you crazy?"

"People are complicated organisms," he says as he wrinkles his brow.

"Does that make Jade and Hannah oxy…what-ever you said?"

"Jade and Hannah seem like opposites," he says.

"Got that right," I say.

"Do you like her?"

"Who? Hannah?" I frown as I grab my math book. Like her? "We have nothing in common," I say.

"You're both…girls?"

I laugh. "Isn't that like having something in common with half the world?"

"Jade's a girl too but…I don't know." He shakes his head and reaches for a book. "A paradox is where two facts are opposite each other," he says. "Like…someone who claims to be a friend while doing mean things."

He looks straight at me with his serious eyes. I turn away and rumble through more junk in my locker. My head is already too full without Russell's para-whatever.

An announcement blasts into the hall from the Broadcaster.

Roads on the parade route will be closed this week to complete preparations for the floats.

Now the parade is something worth talking about. "Are you on a float, Russell?" I ask.

He shakes his head, no. "I guess I'll go and watch."

"Will you wave to me?" I ask with a big smile. "If you stand near the curb, I'll be able to find you in the crowd and wave back. I swing my arms back and forth to demonstrate, and we both laugh. "Maybe stand near Central Street?"

"Okay," he says with a wide grin.

My respond-pad beeps that the math review has started, but I don't want my good mood to end, and besides, I'm starving.

Lunch seems a much better idea. I shut my locker and start down the hall.

"Hey, Jenny?" Russell calls after me. "Hannah might turn out…I don't know…you might like her," he says.

I shrug and head toward the cafeteria. Russell is not smart about everything.

The cafeteria isn't crowded. I sit down at an empty table and pull out my lunch from my backpack. The Broadcaster plays a song from a cool band and then switches to a teen model telling us to wear red—a great color for everyone—to the parade. Maybe that red top would look good on me. Then there's an ad that shows a boy using the Math Tutor program and bragging about how easy it is to use. I bet it's been upgraded. I pull up the algebra assignment on my respond-pad. X and Y variables stare back at me. I still don't understand the directions.

"If you're a genius at both math and respond-pad programming, I can't sit here."

I look up and there he is. Kyle.

"I suck at math," I say feeling my face heat.

"So…can I…is anybody?" He points to the empty table.

"Sure," I say.

"Be right back." He puts his backpack down and heads for the food line.

My hands shake as I sneak out my mirror. My hair is okay; no food in my teeth. *He's just a person,* I tell myself. A person. I can talk to people. I can talk to people. What did the health teacher say in our relaxation unit? Inhale and count, or was it exhale and count? I try both.

"I'm mad at you, but I guess I'll sit here anyway." Jade drops her stuff next to mine. "Whose junk is that?"

No. This can't be happening. She's going to ruin it. If anyone asks me to explain what a panic attack feels like, I'd say you feel hot and cold at the same time and the air around changes to a poison that you can't breathe. Your heart starts some race that requires it to try to jump out of your chest.

"Did you hear me?" Jade asks.

"You can't sit here," I say. "I'm doing math with someone."

"Who?"

"No one."

"It's your stupid buddy," Jade smirks.

"Yeah. It's a buddy meeting, and no one can be around." Air comes back into my lungs. "Sorry," I continue. "You don't want to be stuck talking to her, do you?"

"Stuck talking to who?" Kyle asks as he sits.

Jade glares at me and then gives Kyle her movie-star smile. "I'm Jade. You're Kyle from the debate team?" she asks in this soft voice I don't recognize. "I love debate. You're sooo good."

Kyle shrugs and says, "Thanks."

Jade has never been to a debate and wouldn't even know Kyle was on the team if I hadn't told her. I want to say this out loud, but I sit like a dummy.

Kyle turns to me. "Debate is easier than math," he says.

He says this so casually, I relax enough to say, "I don't get algebra problems. And if you think X means one thing but it doesn't, everything you do after is wrong."

"There's no real answer in debate," Kyle says. "You adjust as things change. It's all about using facts to make the best argument."

"Facts can be fun," Jade pipes in. "Do you know there will be twenty-four bands in the parade?"

My throat tightens.

"My father – he works for Governcorp – says the floats will be the best ever, and prizes for people riding on them are amazing." Jade opens her eyes wide and smiles again at Kyle.

He nods and then concentrates on his sandwich.

"I've got a brand-new Protector," she says as she takes it out of her purse and twists it around her finger. She hasn't taken her eyes off Kyle yet. He takes a quick look at the Protector but then concentrates on his sandwich. He takes three large bites.

Jade's not finished. "I have a great idea, Kyle," she says as she puts her Protector away.

I feel like I'm watching a movie. The next scene is where the girl touches the boy's arm and smiles again and reminds him they are meant to be together forever or at least on the Ferris wheel in the parade. The girl will get what she wants.

"It's about the parade." Jade moves her chair closer to Kyle.

Kyle looks at her and takes one more bite of the sandwich, and then instead of answering, he chokes. He coughs and signals for a drink. When Jade and I both reach out to grab the cup, our hands collide, and the cup topples over, flooding soda across the table. Jade scoots away as fast as possible, but not before the sticky liquid soaks her skirt.

"You ruined it!" she yells at me. She wipes at the skirt again and again with a napkin. "You clumsy…you… Barf Head!" She stomps away to the bathroom.

I'm relieved Kyle has stopped coughing. He gets a drink from the fountain, and then comes back and helps me wipe up the mess with napkins. I'm afraid to even glance at him. He must think I'm a klutz.

He throws away the napkins then says, "Wasn't very nice of her to call you a Barf Head."

I touch my hair, cursing it and Hannah Cossack.

"You have…" He smiles. "You have nice hair."

My cheeks grow warm, and my heart speeds up, but this time it's the best feeling ever.

I smile back. "Thanks," I say.

We sit down again. My stomach turns somersaults, and the only thing I can eat are some potato chips. I don't even know where to look. At Him? At the chips? Why can't the Broadcaster shut up a minute? When will I think of something to say?

"I want to know how you got a perfect score on programming," Kyle says as he finishes my chips.

This is what he mentioned during the assembly when he picked up my respond-pad. "I didn't cheat," I say.

"Sorry, I didn't mean it that way," he blushes. "Don't tell anyone," he leans closer to me and whispers, "but I'm jealous." He smiles, and I feel a magical tingling up and down my spine.

I smile back. "It's the same programming language as viewers," I explain. "I get a lot of practice in the safety office."

"You go to the safety office?"

"My mom is the Middletown officer."

Kyle gives me a puzzled look.

"What?" I ask.

"Nothing. Programming viewers?"

I shrug. "Doesn't help with algebra."

He laughs. "Nothing helps with algebra."

I smile through all the rest of my classes and avoid Jade. I see her, and my other friends walk toward the Buying Center after school, and I tell myself I don't care. My mom will be glad to see me in the safety office.

***

"You're late again," my mom yells the second I walk in the door.

"I came right after..."

"Monitor these viewers while I look up some data," she says without looking at me. "Reliable Carmichael took the day off."

I put away my backpack and watch people pass on North Street, then Cramer, then Mayfield, and then Stratford. The viewers scan one block after another without stopping unless something looks unusual. My mom bends over her desk, her fingers hitting the respond-pad keys again and again. The wrinkles on her forehead used to disappear when she stopped staring at the screens, but now they last – just like her angry moods. She always thinks of work. Nothing but work.

The Broadcaster talks about a butterfly and a lost gerbil and a man throwing away burned chocolate-chip cookies. He was making them for his daughter. At least he was trying. "Mom," I say. "Let's make the cupcakes you love tonight. We just need to go to the store."

I look up the recipe on my respond-pad.

"Does that sound good? Mom?"

"What?" she says.

"You're not listening."

"The agreement is, you come here to help and not be disrup-tive. How many people on the forty-five-hundred block of York?"

"How many people should there be?" I ask.

"Don't answer a question with a question. It's rude. Count, then log in the number. It's important."

I want to say, "It's not important to me," but I just do what she asks.

My mind drifts to Kyle. Is there a chance he might like me and not Jade?

Why else would he have asked to sit with me today? The Broadcaster says never let a boy break up a friendship, but it also says a real friend doesn't cause a couple to break up. Kyle and I aren't a couple. But Jade and Kyle aren't either.

"What happened to the viewer?" My mom is standing over the monitor that shows pictures from viewer twenty-three. The screen is empty and black.

"Why aren't you paying attention?" She tries all the knobs and controls. "It's covered up," she mumbles. "Somebody threw something at it, and then ran." She gets aspirin out of her drawer.

I sit for a while, and then ask, "Will you arrest the person?"

"The viewer didn't ID them, and you weren't watching." Her voice is almost a whisper, which makes me feel worse than if she had yelled.

"I'm sorry."

"Just finish your homework."

She slumps down and, for a minute, she looks too old to be my mom.

I get my stuff and move to the desk. I didn't know that some criminal would knock out the viewer. I want to ask why she can't take a break and help me with my homework for a change instead of worrying about dumb opportunity people and protesters, but I know I just have to try harder.

"When I'm an officer, I'll memorize all the answers and know how to do everything right," I say. "I'll get a hundred percent on every test."

I don't think she hears me. At least Kyle was impressed.

On the desk, I notice an old picture of my mom and me relaxing at the community pool. We're both smiling. When she was in law school, we'd go to the park and have picnics and take walks. If I could just be a better helper. I pull out the respond-pad and log in. I have another buddy report due. The questions are getting tougher.

"Now that you are friends with your buddy, you will want to get to know more about her. Have a friendly conversation using these prompts and turn in your answers."

Who are your buddy's other friends?
Jade, Trix, and Sable

How much time does she spend with them?
After school, most days. She goes to fashion club too.

Does your buddy ever visit the Homestead? Does she have friends there?
No. No.

Is your buddy excited about participating in the parade?
Yes, very excited.

What is your buddy's favorite subject?
Monkeys.

I read the question again. Maybe they mean favorite school subject.
~~**Monkeys**~~**. Math.**

How can anyone's favorite subject be math? Maybe I should change that one again.

I look up and watch a girl show off a cute hairstyle on the Broadcaster. I find my mirror and hairbrush and decide to copy it. Would Kyle like it a new way? "Do you think I have nice hair? Mom?"

"Hmm?" she says without looking.

"Do you like this style?"

Her Governcorp pager activates. She closes her eyes a second and clears her throat before she answers.

"Morgan." She makes her voice sound strong and confident. "A few pranks. Nothing out of the ordinary." She walks back and forth across the room. "My plan?" She takes a deep breath and says, "My plan is to book someone before the parade and make an example." Her boss asks more questions, but after a few minutes, my mom hangs up and then sighs.

I look down at my work because I know I'm not supposed to listen to conversations, but she surprises me with a hug.

"I just need you to hang in there until after the parade," she says.

I nod.

"And you know I think you have the prettiest hair on the planet." She smiles and looks like herself again.

"Will I have to cut my hair short like yours when I'm an officer?"

She shakes her head no.

"Boys like long hair," I say without thinking.

"A boy likes your hair?" she says back.

"I didn't say that."

She smiles.

"Unfair," I say. "You knew what I was thinking."

She stands behind me, picks up my brush, and brushes my hair like she did when I was little. "I wish I could read your mind," she says. "I just use deductive reasoning."

"What's that?"

"Using information to draw a logical conclusion. You asked a random question about your hair, then about boys, and I put them together."

I hold up the mirror and see both our faces together. Two, but not three.

"Was my dad your first boyfriend?"

"No. I met him in college."

"Was he hot?"

She laughs, but her eyes look sad at the same time. She puts down the brush.

"Switch places," I say. She hesitates but surprises me by doing what I ask. I brush her light brown hair until I can see she's relaxed again. "Do you miss him?" I say just above a whisper.

She looks over at the picture of me when I was little. "Sometimes when I remember things we did together, I miss the good feelings," she says.

I need to ask the one question. The question buried deep in my head and my heart. But like every time before, I'm afraid.

My mom takes my hand. "He loves you very much."

"No," I argue. "He never came back." The words choke in my throat, and I decide I don't need to ask the question. I know the answer already. "He left because of me," I say. "He can't love me." I turn around, and tears flow down my cheeks.

My mom hugs me from behind and doesn't say anything for a minute.

"Don't believe that, Jenny," she says in her soft voice. "Never believe that." Her voice makes me want to change my mind. "Life is complicated," she says and holds me close. "Your dad and I saw things in different ways. I tried to convince him. He tried to convince me. He was stubborn."

"Like you," I say.

"Like you," she says and tussles my hair.

I face her again. "What did he want to convince you about?"

"It's hard to explain. When grandpa and all those people watching the soccer game got killed, the whole country got scared. People were in a panic and wanted something or someone to tell them what to do. They wanted more than anything to feel safe again. Your dad didn't like the people who got elected. They made a lot of changes. They built the Homesteads. They decided citizens should protect themselves more."

"Those are good things," I say.

"That's what I decided," my mom says.

"You stopped being a lawyer and became a safety officer," I say.

"Yes," she nods. "Sometimes people look at a problem and come up with different solutions."

"Then one answer's wrong," I say. "Like math."

She hugs me again. "Then one answer's wrong," she repeats. "Sit down a minute."

I sit in the chair next to her, and she leans close to me. "My boss doesn't like me much, and I really don't like him," she says.

"Mom, I know that."

"But I believe in what I'm doing."

"Me, too," I say.

"Keeping people safe at the parade is important to me," she says. "I need to arrest anyone who might be a threat. You can help."

"Watching the viewers?"

"At school," my mom says. "My boss thinks students will cause trouble. He says it's my fault that some asked controversial questions at the assembly."

"It wasn't your fault."

"I guaranteed that you would report anyone suspicious and that you will do a perfect job with your buddy."

I swallow hard as I nod.

"I'm just so glad I can count on you." She smiles and hugs me again.

The Broadcaster in her office rings out loud and clear.

Clouds cause rain. Do rabbits dig the holes in my grass? I saw one go down the hole. The parade will have protesters. Everyone loves a parade.

Hannah

I'm up early to write in my journal.

Ways to Make Money

I list babysit, dog sit, and fast food, and realize that's my whole list. For other jobs, I need to be out of school. I would never talk my parents into that. I log into my respond-pad and search for "Protector permit" information. The pages keep rerouting me to Protector ads and warnings about deadlines until at last, I find an article from an anti-Governcorp blog that says permits to be without a Protector are sometimes called yearly fines and vary by city, but the average is 60,500 tokens. What? Even someone with a high-paying job would take years to save that much. Kyle's must be counterfeit. What is he thinking?

I start a new heading on the next page of my journal.

Things I can do to make my life better now.

Good heading. I write:

Read a book.
Take a walk.
Go to the zoo.

I underline the last one. I haven't been there in ages. I think again about the monkeys that escaped. I wish I could interview the four who ran away. Do you like your freedom? Are you happier? Will you take me with you?

I straighten my monkey figurines. Mrs. Koboyashi gave me my first one when we came to the Homestead. The figurine had such exquisite detail that I asked if the monkeys were real. "They are very real to me," she said. "Three wise monkeys come from Japan's golden rule," she explained. "Do not see more than you should, do not hear more than is necessary, and do not talk when you have no need."

"What does that mean?" I asked.

"It means you are polite if you live in Japan." She wrapped my hand around the figurine. "You keep it."

I miss Mrs. Koboyashi. I pull Shizaru from my shelf. He is a black, marble figure that sits alone in a lotus position with his arms folded. The fourth monkey. He stands for "Do no evil." See no evil, hear no evil, speak no evil, do no evil. Are the monkeys being polite—like Mrs. Koboyashi said—or are they denying the world around them? Is that a form of evil, too? I push away the thought. Maybe I'm selfish; maybe I don't want to deal with flyers or protests. Maybe I just want to be left alone and take care of myself and get through life. And if I'm not doing anything wrong, maybe that's all the world gets. Maybe I just want to be a good enough citizen.

The Broadcaster blares out, telling me cicadas make noise, and someone has dirty sunglasses, but they don't know how to clean them. "Why do you turn this up?" I mumble under my breath to whoever the offending household member might be. I turn the machine down on my way to the kitchen.

"I need to be early today," my mom says as she gulps some coffee. "Would you...?" She points to Emma and Lily.

I nod.

"Bus in five," she says as she kisses my sisters and me, and then goes out the door.

I help Emma and Lily find their backpacks, and then we watch for the bus out the living room window. They begin to hum. It's a catchy tune. A new hit I haven't heard? "What's that song?"

"You know," Lily says.

I shake my head no.

"The Safety Song!" they both shout out. Then they sing.

"Careful watch night and day,
Viewers make it safe to play.

Finger Stamps are good and fine,
Never have to wait in line.

When I'm big, I will know,
Who is friend and who is foe?

Viewers and Protectors help us.
Keep us all so safe."

They laugh and start all over. I feel my lip curl, and I shake my head as they sing. Lily stops and cocks her head. "Did we do it wrong?" She looks up at me, unsure of what to do next.

I can't speak.

"Bus!" Emma shouts from near the window. They race down the stairs for the door.

"We'll practice!" Lily yells back.

"Don't," I mumble as the door slams. "Please, don't."

The sound of a woman's horrible laugh makes me turn to the Broadcaster. The woman has on a nurse's uniform. She stands next to a man about my parents' age. His eyes don't focus, and he sways. His smile is as fake and big as the Cheshire cat's. The woman cackles again and pats the man's arm as she talks. "This is Bob," she says. "He was rejuvenated at the Comfort Center after he got sick. He looks great."

I can't listen to this. The remote? I look on the sofa, under a pillow left on the floor, the chair, and on the table. Where is the remote?

"Bob is doing great," the woman continues.

Where!?

"Gov…ern…Govern…corp." Bob struggles to get the words out. "Thank you for well." The man raises his left lip towards his cheek in a bizarre half smile.

"It was our pleasure to make you well, Bob," the woman says.

And then the two figures are gone. Someone flies a drone over a pond.

Will lemon bubble gum turn your teeth yellow?

It's over. Never happened. Bob, who are you? Who were you? You were never sick. You did something against Governcorp and you were put on the Broadcaster as a reminder of what can be done to people. I lost Mrs. Koboyashi when she was sent to the Comfort Center. What if it's Kyle or Maria or Jonah one day?

I throw up, and then I go to school.

***

It's been almost three weeks, but the corridors still look alike to me. I round a corner, and once again, I'm lost in the Decider section. Kyle sees me and leads me out of the maze.

"Need more flyers?" he asks under his breath.

"No."

"It's all legal."

"I just want to be left alone."

"The constitution guarantees peaceful assembly."

"What about the Comfort Centers?"

"What do they have to do with…?

"Have you heard the Safety song?" I stop in the middle of the hall.

"Did you see Bob this morning?" I ask.

"Who? What?" Kyle leads me to a corner.

The worse case scenarios flood through my head as I lean against the wall.

"You will end up in the Comfort Center for nothing," I say.

"What we're doing is totally legit," he insists.

"How about your 'legit' Protector permit?" I say with air-quotes.

"Take the blindfold off, Hannah. You know how bad things are."

Not as bad as in the Comfort Center, I think.

"Sometimes you just have to chance it," he says.

"Hi, Kyle." Jade comes out of nowhere and interrupts us. Her voice is like a cat's whine. She places her body between Kyle and me. I consider growling.

"I have a little invite," she says as she puts an envelope in a loop on Kyle's backpack. "Let me know if you can make it," she purrs. "Talk soon."

Kyle nods as she walks away.

"Jeez," he says when she's out of earshot.

"Think it's your wedding invitation?"

"Shut up." He rips open the envelope and reads. "I'm invited to a pre-parade party and to be Jade's guest on the Governcorp Fun Float. A seat on the Ferris wheel."

We laugh, but then I wonder if we should be joking.

"Don't you see?" I say as we walk down the hall. "Her father works for Governcorp."

"Lots of people work for Governcorp."

"Forget about protesting the parade, Kyle. Let things go for now and think about your future."

"My future depends on changing things now. You should see that."

"Your argument is third rate."

Kyle stiffens, then he tears up the invitation and tosses it in a nearby trash can. He picks up his pace, and I hurry to catch up. We walk in silence until the Developer lockers come into view.

"Thanks for walking me through the maze again," I say.

We stop and size each other up. Our friendship goes too deep for us to be mad for very long.

"I get the most satisfaction when I change the minds of the head-strong adjudicators," Kyle says with a raised brow. He turns to go but notices Jenny up ahead at her locker. "What do you think of your buddy?" he asks.

"Don't ask."

"Who does she like?"

"Are you serious?"

He smiles and shrugs.

I want to say, "take the blindfold off" and remind him Jenny's mother enforces the laws but I'm tired of arguing. I punch him with my book instead.

"I'm skipping class this afternoon," he laughs. "Jonah will be down the street at the park. Come?"

My heart jumps a beat and yells, Yes, Yes, Yes!

But my brain wins, and I wave goodbye as he walks out the door.

Jenny

I have my list ready as I wait at the lockers for Hannah. I'll check her Protector holder and find out her favorite school subject and remind her the parade is only days away and she must be at the float-staging site early. My mom will not be disappointed.

Everything will be fine. I'm doing my job.

Hannah finally shows up. "What took you so long?" I ask.

"Are you waiting for me?"

"Don't answer a question with a question. It means you're rude."

"I got lost," Hannah says. "The Decider hall looks just like this one."

"Follow the group," I explain. "Most people know how to do that."

"Yep," she says as she rolls her eyes and turns away to get her books.

"What do you mean?" I say.

"What do you think I mean?"

"You did it again."

"Answering a question with a question means a person is smart," she says.

"It means a person doesn't know the answer."

"Few questions have exact answers."

"Answers are always right or wrong," I say, chin tilted up. "Yes or No. True or false. Even little kids know they have to choose the right answer."

"Sometimes a choice could be right or wrong, depending," Hannah says raising her eyebrows.

Why does this girl say weird things and drive me nuts?

The viewer speaker blasts a loud announcement that no one expects. "All students go to your locker. All students to the lockers immediately."

Kids pour into the locker area. Hannah's face goes pale, and her eyes grow wide as she whispers, "What's going on?"

Governcorp officials gather at the end of the hallway, and in a nanosecond, I recognize the short, fat man. I feel my heart racing as I turn my face into my open locker.

"What?" Hannah says in a panic.

"Just follow instructions. That man is Vince Flakeman, and I don't want him to see me."

"Have your Protectors ready to show," his voice booms.

I wipe my sweaty hands on my skirt, close my eyes, and then take a deep breath. Just walk by, Mr. Skunk. Just walk by, please.

Hannah

The sound of lockers opening is eerie without kids talking and laughing in the background. My mind and heart race. Am I supposed to know who Vince Flakeman is? He's asking to see Protectors? I tell myself to be calm; use logic. The law says I don't have to have the Protector with me right now. It's okay that I left it at home. It's the law.

We stand like silent statues as this man, Flakeman, walks the hall. His icy stare lands periodically on a student, and without speaking, he sticks out his hand for the person's Protector. The eerie quiet is interrupted only when he decides to search a locker and then shuts it with a bang. I try to figure out if he stops in front of people who look scared or those who look proud to show off their prized possession. I'd mimic the right pose to be passed over, but there's no pattern. I just try to breathe and stare at the floor.

Flakeman breaks his silence when he inspects a Protector from a scrawny boy with a shaved head. "What's your name?" he asks.

"Mason," the boy says.

"Let's play a little game, Mason," Flakeman says as he rubs his hands together. "You." He points at a girl. "You be our intruder. Go down the hall and then walk back toward us. Point your Protector at Mason."

The girl follows directions. When she gets ten feet away from Mason, Flakeman tells her to stop. The color in Mason's face disappears.

"What's the matter, Mason?" Flakeman says with his palms up. "If she were a real intruder, you'd shoot, right?" Flakeman turns Mason around to face his locker. "Shoot the locker," he says. "Show all your classmates how you would protect them." I see Mason's lip quiver. "Now!" Flakeman yells. Mason holds an old-style Protector that uses bullets. He pulls the trigger, but nothing happens. It isn't loaded.

"Stand in the middle of the hall," Flakeman orders.

Mason wipes tears with his sleeve and does as he is told. His legs wobble, and his Protector hand shakes. I look down at my feet. Flakeman goes around the corner to the other set of lockers. It seems like hours pass. Mason might as well be standing naked he seems so vulnerable.

I whisper to Jenny, "Who is that man?" She shakes her head because Flakeman reappears.

"Where's the prize-winner?" he asks.

The words hit me like a punch in the stomach. Prize-winner. I feel my knees go weak, but I force myself to stand straight and tall when a girl points me out. Vince Flakeman looks me in the eye.

"So, you're Hannah." He raises the edge of his lip into a fake smile.

He's short with a neck that looks like a stub plopped on top of his shoulders, and his Governcorp jacket reaches only halfway around his protruding stomach. His eyes are black and bulging like an insect's. Tufts of hair protrude from behind his ears and point up like horns. He's a cartoon villain come to life. "I'm glad you are well today," he says.

It takes me a minute to realize he's referring to the fake sickness reports Jenny sends in to avoid going to buddy meetings. What else does he know?

"How are things going?" He looks at Jenny.

"Fine," Jenny says.

"Your high math scores are surprising," he says to me. "Is your buddy helping you?"

Out of the corner of my eye, I see Jenny grimace.

"She teaches me a lot," I say.

"Hmm. And who are your friends?"

Does he know I saw Maria? If I mention Kyle, will he get in trouble?

"Jenny has introduced me to people," I say. I feel sweat start on the back of my neck.

"And who might they be?" he asks with that fake smile again.

My brain goes blank, and the few seconds that pass seem like an hour. I feel everyone's eyes on me.

"I'm a great friend of yours," says the boy next to me. "I'm Russell, sir." Flakeman bends his head back to glance up at the six-foot-five boy with the huge arms. He ignores Russell's outstretched hand.

My brain is working again.

"Jade is another person I know," I say. "And, of course, Jenny."

He turns to Jenny. "Only students who enforce and follow the laws are allowed into the Academy. We follow things closely."

"I understand, sir," Jenny says without blinking.

Flakeman turns back to me. "Do you know Kyle Foster?"

Does he know the truth? If I lie, will he arrest me? Can he do that? I think of my dad. I know what he would want me to do.

"Yes. I know who he is," I say. I can tell by the scowl on Flakeman's face that he expected me to lie. "How is it that you know…"

"Kyle Foster?" Russell says. "He's the guy in debate. Everybody knows him."

I look at Russell. His glasses are half-off. The blotch on his right cheek is a bout of acne starting. His shirt sticks out, and his jeans stop way too high above his tennis shoes. He may be the first boy I kiss.

Flakeman's scowl grows deeper. "Why isn't your Protector in a holder?"

Before I can answer, he turns my backpack upside down. I hold in a gasp as the protest forms fall out.

"Why do you have these?" he snarls. "Where did you get them?"

I must think logically. Kyle says they are legal, but I don't want to mention his name. Can I say I found them?

"These are simple questions, Miss Cossack, for someone who seems so smart."

"That was one of my assignments," Jenny says, firm and clear.

Flakeman and I turn in surprise.

"I asked Hannah to pick up any forms floating around in the school so I can take them to my mother."

Flakeman rips the forms to pieces. "Everyone at the parade will be a happy citizen or a grateful opportunity person." He turns to address all the students. "Understand me?" Everyone nods. He throws my backpack on the floor. "Where's the Protector?"

Don't panic, I tell myself despite my racing pulse. He can bully me, but I know the law says I don't have to carry it yet. I just tell the truth.

"I left it at home," I say plainly.

"She forgot it," Jenny adds.

A normal person would nod or look embarrassed or say sorry. A normal person would cower to this intimidation. But what good is it to go from an opportunity person to a citizen if you're just as frightened as ever by Governcorp?

I lift my chin. "The deadline to carry a Protector is a week away," I say.

"Is that so?" He spits the words out like they're poison. His eyes have such fury; I think he might grab me and throw me on the floor, or worse.

"That was on the Broadcaster this morning," Russell says.

Flakeman pauses but doesn't look at Russell.

"Middle of the hall," Flakeman says to me.

I clench my jaw and move next to Mason. If I cry, it will be from anger, not out of fear of this wretched man. Flakeman goes behind the girl who plays the role of an intruder. He raises her arm.

"Fall when I point the Protector at you," he orders the students around us.

Students fall one by one—some of them enjoying the drama of the game. Then Flakeman takes the girl's Protector and walks to where Mason and I stand. He points the Protector right at us, and Mason falls to the floor in a ball. The sound of his crying is magnified by the silence of everyone else. A second later I feel the Protector against my head. I press my elbows against my side and freeze.

"I don't care that the intruder killed you," Flakeman hisses. "But you let fellow citizens die." He sweeps his arm in a grand gesture toward all the students playing dead. He looks down his nose at Mason and then glares at me. "What kind of people are you?"

I'm not breathing. What will he do next? I flinch as his pager goes off. He swears, gives the Protector back to the girl and then turns to me. "I don't have time for you right now," he says. "But you are on my mind, Miss Cossack. There will be some changes especially for you."

He turns his scrunched face to Jenny. "Good luck with your Academy application," he snips. "You'll need it."

I shiver as he marches out the door.

Jenny

I won't let my tears show. I won't. I stare inside my locker and listen as kids scramble to leave or shout to each other about their "dead man" performance. I hear Hannah help Mason up off the floor.

"That man is a monster," she says.

I'd like to tell her I call him Mr. Skunk, and I hate the way he treats my mom, and sometimes I pretend his face is the target during my Protector practice. I want to say I know he's horrid and he does mean and terrible things to everyone, but I need to be an officer. I swallow down the lump in my throat and turn around. The hall is empty except for Hannah and Mason.

"Vince Flakeman is my mom's boss and an important Governcorp official," I say. "Go home, Mason, and fix your Protector. Stop being a baby."

"Shut, up," Hannah snaps. "He had no right to do that."

I ignore her and get books out of my locker. Mason leaves, and Hannah picks up the contents of her backpack, which Flakeman dumped on the floor.

"Don't ever leave your Protector home again," I say. "And get a holder."

"I'll find a way to pay, so I don't ever have to carry it again," Hannah says.

"No one does that."

"I'm not riding in the parade either."

"You can't cause trouble," I say. My voice comes out shaky this time. My head is swimming. My mom will lose her job because I'm a failure. "You have to follow the rules, or I'll report you," I say.

"Report how you copy your math from Jade and how you make up information. On parade day, report that I'm sick," Hannah says. "I'm sick a lot, right?"

"Only stupid people would complain about a parade," I yell back, my heart beating fast again. "And you don't want to go to buddy meetings any more than I do. If you would send me your work like you're supposed to, my reports would be right."

"Leave me alone, Jenny."

I watch as Hannah cleans up the mess. How did she say those things to Vince Flakeman? I would have stammered and mixed up my words and, even though I hate to admit it, probably cried. Hannah didn't even say anything bad about me. But still, I'm in trouble because she won't cooperate.

"Are you passing out protest flyers?"

"Kyle says they're legal," Hannah answers.

"Kyle. You really know Kyle?"

"We're friends from the Homestead."

"Kyle never lived in the Homestead," I argue. "He's not an opportunity person."

"You always think I'm lying." Hannah walks toward the door. "But you better believe this: on parade day, I will be very sick. Everyone in the whole school has been witness to my touchy stomach."

"Governcorp won't believe you if I say it's not true." I narrow my eyes at her. "Do you want officials to come to your house and deport your family?"

"I'm following the law," Hannah says, but her voice isn't strong and confident anymore.

I have to think of something. Maybe I can find some reason for her to miss the parade. Why do I care if she's there or not? I'd have more fun without her anyway. I just need her to have that Protector.

"If you put your Protector in a holder and have it on you every day, I'll officially get you out of riding on the float."

"How?"

"I'll come up with a good excuse."

"Why?"

"You ask too many questions."

"I'll think about it," she says.

"I need your math and other homework, too."

"Forget it."

My heart is racing in panic. She has to cooperate. I need to tell her something that will scare her as much as it scares me.

"I don't want to be on the bad side of Vince Flakeman. Do you?"

Hannah

My stomach churns with thoughts of Vince Flakeman. Jenny is right. I don't want to face him again. I rush home and screen Kyle.

"Flakeman is all bluff," Kyle says.

"You didn't see him," I say. "He's capable of anything. He must know you're passing out those protester forms."

"And I just picked up some more."

"No, don't," I warn.

"Look. I'm sorry he did that to you," he says with a new calm in his voice. "Flakeman thinks he's above the law, but no person is. People forget they have rights," he says. "I will never forget mine."

"He knew things about me—he asked about you," I say. "I think he's been watching me. Maybe watching you."

"They watch everyone, Hannah. You just have to care enough to make them stop," Kyle says. "Join us."

I shake my head and disconnect the call without saying good-bye. I'll never persuade him. I need to think.

Everything is better at the zoo.

***

I head straight for the monkeys. I push pieces of bananas through the bars. They take the pieces as quick as they can and then run away. One monkey hides by a tree. I coax him, but he won't come. He tilts his head; I tilt mine. He scratches his head; I scratch mine. He rubs his nose; I rub mine. He comes closer.

"Of the two hundred sixty known monkey species, capuchins are known to be some of the smartest; they make and use tools and teach skills to their young."

Startled, I turn and see that the science lesson has come from Russell. He leans his face on the bars.

"You left school so fast, I didn't get a chance to tell you…"

"He's coming back." Russell points to the monkey.

The monkey scratches his ear. I scratch mine and then hold out the banana. He inches up and watches me watching him. I hold out the banana, and he grabs it.

"A primate feels secure after he watches you, especially if you imitate him," Russell says.

"You know a lot about monkeys."

"Not so much." He kicks some rocks and dirt. He's much more comfortable looking at the ground than at me.

"Thanks for today," I say. "It was brave."

He shrugs.

The monkey chatters, and we both watch it run away. Russell keeps his eyes on the monkey but says, "Do you like your new school?"

"Not really." I gasp because had no intention of confessing such a thing. It just slips out—maybe because we aren't looking at each other or maybe because Russell rescued me today. I glance around, checking for a viewer; I've talked too much again.

"It's broken," Russell says.

"What?"

"The viewer. Over there on the light post."

I look up high and see wires sticking out of a small hole.

"The 6DVX wire installation got hit by lightening, but I pulled out some wires just in case. Being tall comes in handy sometimes." He shrugs again but this time looks at me.

"You dismantled it?" I whisper this even though he just told me no one can hear. "Wasn't that dangerous?"

He shrugs again. "I like the idea of a private place." He puts his hands in his pockets and shuffles more stones. The Broadcaster blares nearby.

I like honey. Do bees still make it? Where's my favorite sock? Things disappear if you don't pay attention. Sunlight tomorrow. Everyone loves the parade. Join your friends for fun. Get a Flex-o-matic Protector; now on sale everywhere. Your color is available. Send us the news.

"Still kind of noisy," he says.

We both laugh, then he looks down again.

"I don't want to see you or Jenny get in trouble." He kicks a few more stones and then takes off running. He stumbles and recovers enough to yell back, "Good to be your friend, Hannah."

I look over at the wires. "Thanks for everything, Russell," I yell back as loudly as possible.

I walk home and play a game with myself. How many sounds can I hear that don't come from the Broadcaster? A plane. A robin? Maybe a cardinal. A baby crying. Natural sounds can't compete with the constant jabber. I pull out my respond-pad. If I have to listen to it, I'll let it say my message for a change. I'm near a park, so I find a bench and send two sentences. As I wait for my message to play on the nearby Broadcaster I watch two parents with their kids; their laughing and giggling make me smile. An older couple walks their dog. A man jogs. How many of you wish for a private place, like Russell? How many of you would report a broken viewer to Governcorp to be repaired? The Broadcaster sounds.

Jobs available at Your Diner. Flash your speedy pass at any Broadcaster to apply. Citizens only.

I applaud the monkeys who have gained freedom. One day it will be me.

I let my smile widen as I hear my message. One day it will be me.

Jenny

It's dinnertime, and everyone else's mom is cooking in the kitchen. Everyone else's mom is around to talk to. My mom sends a respond-pad message, "Get Pizza." Pizza more than three times in the same week is not fun.

I scan the Broadcaster entertainment channels for shows I can watch only in secret, but even those aren't interesting anymore. My mind drifts to Hannah. If she doesn't cooperate, and I report her, will I be considered a failure? Is that another thing for Vince Flakeman to hold against me—and my mom? Hannah has to cooperate this time. What happens if I let her skip the parade and he finds out? My stomach churns. I need some fun. My mom didn't say where to get pizza. I rush out the door. Everyone will be at the Buying Center, and once we're together having fun, Jade will act like her old self.

The Center is crowded. It seems all the hundreds of six-sided shopping station kiosks are occupied. I head for the area where our group always meets, and I watch for Jade. I stand behind a man–men don't usually take long–and when he leaves the station, I put in my token for fifteen minutes of viewing. The Broadcaster shopper channel appears. From the menu, I choose:

DRESS, BLUE, LOW PRICE RANGE, and TEEN STYLE

In seconds, a dress appears on me in the mirror frame. Ugly. I hit NEXT. Yuck. NEXT. Worse. NEXT. This one is okay. I turn sideways. It's nice. Too bad I'm just looking, but I hit SAVE just in case. I decide to change the menu and look at myself in the Academy blazer, even though I already have mine. I smile at myself in the mirror frame. Perfect. I go back to dresses.

"Are you gonna use this, or not?" a woman says to the person in the kiosk on the opposite side of mine. "You can't just stand here like a dummy."

The first time I came without my mom to the Buying Center, I didn't know how to use the machines, and people yelled at me. It's not fair. I hear the woman complain again. "You won't even buy anything," she says. "They shouldn't let people stand and look."

Don't be such a bully I think as I walk to the other side. "I'll help you," I say to the person in the kiosk.

Hannah Cossack looks up. We're both so shocked we just stand and look at each other.

"Well?" the woman says.

"Is this open?" a girl asks, pointing to my screen.

"No," I reply. "I'm coming." This surprise might work out great. I'll make sure Hannah buys her Protector holder, and besides, if I'm nice to her, she'll owe me. "Just come to my screen," I tell Hannah.

I step back into place, and a dress appears on me in the mirror frame.

I model another choice.

Hannah studies the machine. "They don't give directions."

"You put a token in here for viewing time," I say as I point to the slot. "You get it back if you buy something."

She leans over to look, and I smell her lavender shampoo. Her hair is pulled back in a perfect ponytail. She has just the right amount of lip gloss, and her figure is way better than mine. She looks pretty–she always looks pretty, now that I think about it.

"Do you want to see yourself in this dress?"

"Okay," she says.

I show her where to stand. She jumps as the image of herself in the dress suddenly appears, and we both laugh.

"You never came here with your mom?" I ask.

"No money," she says. "My dad gave me ten tokens today."

Ten tokens will hardly buy anything except a Protector holder, but there is nothing more boring than watching someone mirror-frame that. We should have fun first.

"We'll choose items off the menu: BARGAIN PRICE, TEEN, SKIRT?" I ask.

Hannah nods.

She's amazed as item after item appears on her in the mirror frame.

"That one is super cute," I say as a fitted skirt appears. "But you need to add the right top." I put more choices into the program and watch Hannah. She looks beautiful in new clothes—and not at all like an opportunity kid.

"You don't need more boots, Jade." Sable's voice comes from behind me. I see her and Trix and Jade in the next aisle over. Hannah sees them too. "Let's get Chinese," Trix says. I can tell Jade just pushed the BUY button. Trix has a wad of gum she pulls out of her mouth and plays with. Sable puts a token in another shopping machine just to beat out a younger girl. Jade pushes another BUY button. "This is so boring," I hear her say. "Let's go pick this junk up and eat."

"Thanks for helping," Hannah practically whispers. "I understand it now."

I glance over to Jade and the group again. It would take just a few minutes to meet them over at merchandise pick-up or at the Chinese food area. My mind goes back to everything Russell said about Hannah and Jade. Would I rather have Jade remind me what I should and shouldn't eat, or would I rather stick with Hannah?

"I still have time left on my token," I say to Hannah. "And since I picked an outfit for you, you have to help me pick one. It's only fair."

"Okay."

My token runs out in a second, and I put a new one in without saying anything.

We try on dresses and tops and skirts and shoes and pants. I put in two more tokens. We laugh at the stupid designs and *ooh* and *aah* when we try on designer clothes. I pull up my Academy blazer again.

"What's that?" Hannah asks.

"My uniform for the Academy. I work in the safety office all the time. People have to start careers early to get ahead."

"I'd rather walk in the zoo or read."

"Aren't you afraid you'll get stuck with some terrible job later because you didn't prepare?"

"There are lots of ways to prepare for the future."

"You're funny," I say. And interesting, I think, but I don't say that. "I don't go to the zoo, but I've seen the pandas in China."

"You've been to China?"

"Broadcaster Channel 2012. You could see them, too."

Hannah looks disappointed, so I try to explain. "It's not an extra fee channel. It comes with all the Broadcasters."

"I just think it would be nice to actually go to an exotic place like China or Zambia or Tahiti."

"You'd need a bathing suit in Tahiti," I say. I code in BIKINI. "If you want boys to notice you, try these on."

"Never in a million years," Hannah laughs. "That would make Kyle's eyes bug out, I'm sure, though."

I feel pain in my stomach. "You like him?"

"He's just a friend."

"Jade likes him."

"He would never like Jade."

"You don't know that," I say, wishing she were right anyway.

She sighs. "One day you'll believe the things I say. Ask him yourself."

"I could never do that. My hands sweat just thinking about him, and I could never ask him anything personal, and I can't even hope that he could possibly like me and my hair is always a mess and…Look at my chest!"

Hannah laughs, and then I do too because she doesn't laugh in a mean way; she does it in an I'm-your-friend way.

"Guess you need the *Love Connector*." She says this in the same silly voice from the show.

"You're funny. How do you do that?"

"When you have little sisters, you do strange things."

"I wish I had a sister," I say. "Or a brother." Or a family, I think to myself. I don't even seem to have a mom these days.

The timer beeps on the shopping application. "Are you buying the skirt?" I ask.

"Okay," she says. But before we can press BUY, the machine goes to PAUSE and flashes that an official report will be announced.

Official Report: Governcorp is happy to announce a new deadline. All citizens will have their Protectors tomorrow. We are happy that every qualified citizen will be protected sooner than planned. Congratulations, Middletown!

I won't need to worry now about Hannah having her Protector, but when I see the blood drain from her face, I almost say, "Sorry."

Hannah

The cheap holder for the Protector is snug around my waist. There were no tokens left for the skirt, of course. I check the Protector's OFF switch every few minutes even though it scares me to look at it.

"That looks so nice," Jenny gushes when she sees me at the lockers.

I cringe thinking how a Protector could ever look nice. My dad reminded me this morning that at least I would blend in with the other citizens.

"I'd die to wear a long top, but they make me look stupid. So unfair to be short."

She was talking about my clothes—not the Protector? She looks at me again. "Did you find your classes better?" she asks.

"Better, how?" I say.

"You did it again," she says.

"I guess my brain thinks in questions. You could mean, are the classes more interesting? Are they easier? Were the teachers well prepared? Did the kids talk to me?"

I didn't mean to blurt that last thing, and I poke my face into my locker and pretend I need something from way in the back. Just forget it, Jenny. I don't need your friendship. Just keep your part of our deal and keep me off the parade float like you promised. Walk away now, please.

I can feel her eyes still looking at me, and after a few minutes she says, "What I mean is, did you find the rooms without getting lost?"

"Yes. Thanks." I realize I mean the "thanks" in more than one way.

"I never met a person who likes questions."

"Are questions such a terrible thing?"

We look at each other and laugh. She finally gets a joke.

"I should dare you to not ask a question all day long."

"That would be hard," I say.

The Broadcaster comes on:

Buddy report updates due today.

"I need your math homework," Jenny says. "Do you have it?"

So, this is a buddy conversation for her report?

"Fine," I say. Jenny watches as I response-mail my math to her. "I think you'll find the answers satisfactory." I turn back to my locker feeling my blood boil. Jenny still has her eyes on me. "Is there something else?" I snap.

"Engaging in activities you like will lead to friendships," she says.

"Officer Robot again?" I shake my head.

"No, that's not what I…"

I grab the last things I need from my locker and slam it shut.

"Wait," she says. I turn to glare at her, but her eyes are aimed at her feet.

She hunches over her respond-pad, clenching it to her chest. "Sometimes it's hard for me to say things like I want to."

I shift my weight and then look down at my own feet.

I hear her take a deep breath and then she says, "I hope you don't miss your old friends too much. I hope you make new ones."

She looks at me with gentle eyes. It's the nicest thing she's ever said.

We stand in silence for a minute. I'll help you with the math, if you want," I say. "Tomorrow."

"You will?"

When her face lights up, I have to add, "Kyle's eating outside."

She looks down again and mumbles, "I wouldn't know what to say to him."

"Talk about some band or movie or his favorite food. Think about what the *Love Connection* says." I use my funny voice again and make her laugh. She can be fun to talk with.

"Don't worry so much," I say. "Kyle likes you." Jenny smiles back, and I realize maybe, just maybe, she's not so bad.

Jenny

I take my lunch outside. I see him right away at a table by himself. He's using a respond-pad and he brushes his hair out of his eyes a few times. He has on a nice green-and-white pullover–not just a T-shirt–and he never wears ripped jeans like most other guys. He laughs at someone's joke at the next table, and my heart skips.

I can't do it. I turn around to leave.

"Hey, Jenny," he calls out and waves me over.

I feel my cheeks get warm as I sit down.

"Hi," he says.

"Hi." My heart feels like it's going to pound right out of my chest.

The guys at the next table share a gross joke about cockroaches, and I cringe.

"Appetizing," Kyle says.

I laugh, and then he asks which bands I like and tells me that Brain Dead is way better than Splitting Souls, and I give him a million reasons why he's wrong.

"Maybe you should join the debate team," he smirks.

We smile at each other. I manage to eat a bite of my sandwich.

I rack my brain to think of something new to say when a girl taps Kyle on the shoulder. "You collecting these?" she asks as she holds out a protester form.

I don't understand why she's asking Kyle this, but I hold out my hand. "I'll take it to the safety office."

"Great," Kyle says.

"Protesters are a pain for my mom," I say as I fold up the form.

Kyle is quiet for a minute. "I suppose protesters are a pain for your mom," he says. "She has to sign all the forms and make sure everyone is safe."

He opens his backpack and pulls out more forms. They're filled out – not like the blank ones Hannah had in her backpack yesterday. Kyle wants people to protest?

"I don't understand," I say. "Students can't protest."

"A lot of people want to change things."

"Change what things?"

"Laws that make no sense."

I think about my grandpa and how he died—back before Governcorp. A man who was in the country illegally had robbed someone. The man was arrested, but then he was released from jail because the courts did something wrong. A week later, the same man used an automatic weapon to kill my grandpa and hundreds of others at a soccer game.

"My mother helped change laws that made no sense," I say and put the forms in my backpack. My mom will be proud of me.

"It's the laws NOW that make no sense," Kyle says.

He must be confused, but I don't know how to explain things. I don't want him to think I sound like I'm Officer Robot if I talk about rules and laws.

"Hope your mother approves these right away," he says.

I nod because if I talk, I might cry. Was he just being nice to me, so I'll get my mom to sign protest permits? Worse—he has friends who are protesters? I grab the last form and stuff it into my pocket, and then stand to leave.

"You okay?" he asks.

"I need to meet a teacher. See ya," I choke out.

I run into the teacher's bathroom and lock the door.

I would never like someone who helps people go against the law.

I don't like him anymore.

I don't like him.

I don't...

My chest heaves with a huge sob.

When it's time for the next class, I take some deep breaths, wipe my face with cold water, and leave the bathroom tall and straight. I'll do my job and turn the forms in. Kyle is a troublemaker.

***

Carmichael is alone in the safety office when I show up after school. He has the Broadcaster turned up to the max volume while he's making a sandwich in the break room.

I love my dog. White dogs bark less than brown ones. Fifty-five bands will be on the float. Protectors save lives. Are the monkeys back at the zoo? What's not to like?

"Is that true about dogs?" I ask him when he comes out.

"The Broadcaster just said so, didn't it?"

I start to explain that some things the Broadcaster says are jokes, like red being a color for everyone and broccoli tasting the best on Mondays, but Carmichael is watching the viewers, and I don't want to cause more trouble.

I see a pile of protester permits on my mom's desk. "Is my mom going to approve more of these?" I ask Carmichael.

"Not a chance." He pulls out his deck of cards for his usual practice.

"So, if these people don't have permits, do they stand some-place else?"

"If they show up, Uncle Vince wants them arrested."

"What did they do?"

"It's what they might do that counts," he says.

"Does it matter how old they are?"

"Huh?" He flips more cards over.

"What if a person doesn't understand the law and doesn't know he could get arrested?" I think about all the flyers in my backpack. All of them are from students. Maybe I should just throw them away or give them back to people. If they don't know that all the permits have been given out already, it doesn't seem fair for them to get in trouble. I could give them all back to Kyle.

"Why is it okay if some people protest and not others?" I ask.

"Man! I blew it." Carmichael turns the cards over and starts again.

"You have any gum?" he asks.

I reach into my pocket to get the gum and feel the last form Kyle gave me. I give Carmichael the gum, and he sees the form.

"You found one?" he says, looking at it. "Just put it on the pile."

I decide it's easier to do that than explain. I open the form and see Kyle's name. Why does he want to be a protester? I tell myself it doesn't matter since I don't like him anymore, but I put the form back in my pocket. My mom might ask me where I got it or ask who he is or show it to Vince Flakeman.

"I've got to fix a viewer," Carmichael says. "You want to watch the monitors?"

"Sure."

"Your mom will be back soon. Ask her all that complicated stuff."

After Carmichael leaves, I pull Kyle's form out again. He has nice handwriting. Ugh! What do I care? I have a job to do.

I watch the west side of town, where opportunity families live. A girl drops a scarf in front of Viewer 332. It's a psychedelic paisley print. It's an awesome design. Where did she buy it? I turn on the microphone above the viewer and put on the headphones. My mom will never know.

"Your scarf is so cool," I say. "Where did you get it?"

The girl looks around, startled. I forget no one can see me. "I'm in here," I explain. "Just tell me where the scarf came from."

She backs away.

"Stop. Stop!" I yell. I turn the camera to get a better view. The girl hesitates, and I ask again. "Where did you get the scarf?"

The girl clutches her purse. "I didn't do anything," she says. "Here." She holds out the scarf to the air.

"No. Just tell me what store it's from, and then you can go."
I try to sound like a friend and not a stern official. But I see her
lower lip tremble when she says, "Homestead Goods."

"Okay. Thanks."

The girl darts away. I guess I'd be scared too if an invisible
voice from the safety office asked me questions.

I watch and count people on fifteen streets. I see a few kids I'd
like to talk to, but I might scare them too, and besides my mom
could come in the door any minute.

I glance again at Kyle's form and doodle the letter K to match
his writing. I fill half a page and then remind myself I should
be doing other things – anything but thinking about him. My
respond-pad beeps a message. Hannah has sent me another math
assignment. Good. I can copy her answers instead of Jade's.

I hear Carmichael's voice as he and my mom come in the
door, and I stuff Kyle's form back in my pocket and throw away
the scrap paper.

"I went to pull the trigger, and nothing happened," Carmichael says. "I mean, not a single wave came out." He shakes his
Protector.

"Is that the Protector Jenny dropped?" my mom asks.

"Yeah," he says. "Nothing's made to last."

I wonder if I should apologize, but no one seems to be mad
at me.

My mom takes her Protector off and gives it to Carmichael.
"Use this for now. I've got my original." She finds it in the drawer.
It's the first one she ever owned – an older model that uses bullets.
It was my grandpa's.

"Jenny, anyone tampering with the viewers?" she asks.

I shake my head.

"Good," she says. "How's your math?"

"I'm passing with no problem," I say with my chin up and a
slight nod.

She smiles. I almost forgot she could do that.

"You've worked so hard," she says. "Go home and get dressed
up, and we'll go out for dinner."

"Really? Like we used to?" I ask.
"You deserve it."
Yes, I think. I deserve it.

Hannah

Idread dinnertime. There is nowhere to hide from my dad's school questions and his relentless pleasant attitude.

I haven't told my parents about the Protector inspection, the protest flyers, or that Kyle wants me to join his True Democracy group. Maybe knowing these facts would open my dad's eyes a little, but I doubt it. He embraces citizenship too much. I'd just sound like a whiner, and he would worry – maybe with good reason.

I say "yes" when I should and "fine" and "passing" and don't use the words *miserable, bored,* or *disgusted* out loud, and he doesn't argue when I leave to see Maria. We can't screen–it's only for citizens–but I'd rather talk in person anyway.

The outdoor homestead café is crowded. Maria is quiet, and when she avoids my eyes as she stirs her tea, I can't take it any longer.

"Tell me," I say.

"We got the official notice last week," she says. "Zora was right. Taxes have gone up again. No wage increases. My mom's hours were cut. It's a joke. But not funny."

"I don't know what to say."

"We'll never get out in the next year. My dad is going to have a heart attack from the stress. I'll quit school, but I don't know if I'll make enough money to make a real difference. I'll never get to college."

"You're smart. Maybe my mom..."

"No. It's not fair," Maria continues. "Even if I can do it, others can't." She studies her tea again, then says under her breath, "I joined the True Democracy group."

"Maria? Don't let Kyle talk you into things."

She shakes her head. "I've been thinking about it for a while. Protesting is the only way to get Governcorp's attention."

"You and I will leave the country."

"We don't have any place to go. We have no money."

"You'll put your family in danger," I say.

"Come to a meeting." She says this in a quiet voice with her head down. Then she glances up and teases. "You're the one who taught me to ask questions."

I can't help but smile a little. "I should go to a meeting to ask questions?"

"I'm not saying sign up without reading the fine print."

"Kyle will be there?"

"And Jonah. You remember him? That guy always on the edge?"

"The obnoxiously hot guy...always on the edge?" I smile. It feels good to share.

"Really?" She laughs and shakes her head.

"He's...different," I say.

"He's a tech genius," Maria whispers. "I think he's in charge of something important. People say he's a Monkey."

"A monkey?"

"Shhh."

"Is that what the shirt is?" I ask.

"You've seen the shirts?"

"He had one on," I say.

"They're the symbol for the group."

"Do you trust him?"

"Who can you trust?" she says.

That's a terrible thing to say, I think. But maybe she's right.

"There's a meeting Sunday at four," Maria continues. "Do you know the old brick building on Flag Street?"

"The one that used to be a school?"

"I don't know what it used to be," Maria says. "But True Democracy meets there. Kyle says all the viewers nearby are broken. You'll come?"

A song I like plays on the café speaker, and I use it to change topics. We talk about other people we have in common and my sisters and Maria's family and how good the tea is, and soon we're on the sidewalk ready to head in different directions.

"Do your parents know?" I ask.

"My mom suspects. I think she's secretly supportive, except for being scared that I'll do something dangerous."

"Isn't just being with that group dangerous?"

"I'm living with filth and rodents. My parents sleep on a couch. I have to quit school. I wonder if the heat in the building will work this winter or if I'll get deported to some country I can't even pronounce."

"You didn't answer my question."

Maria looks over at the Broadcaster as we listen to another official announcement.

Official Report: Protesters without permits at the parade will be arrested.

"I live for danger," she says as she rips the Governcorp logo on her napkin in two.

Jenny

I decide the best thing to do is wait until after dinner and ask my mom questions about the parade and protesters and everything I don't understand. But first I want to laugh and have fun with her and pretend there is no Homestead or opportunity people or Vince Flakeman. I have on my favorite dress, and I'm drying my hair section by section, so it turns out straight. I wonder if Kyle would like my hair like this? Why do I think about him? My arms are killing me. I turn off the dryer and hear Jade's voice in the living room. She wants to make up! I run to meet her.

"Jade, you're coming too?" I ask.

When I see my mom's face, I know something's wrong.

"Thank you very much, Jade," my mom says.

"I just want to do the right thing, Mrs. Morgan. Or should I call you, Officer Morgan? Anyway, it was very hard, but Jenny means everything to me."

"What are you talking about?" I ask.

Jade turns around. Her eyes are red. "It was to protect you, Jenny. I love you."

She gives me a quick hug then leaves. She's making crying noises outside the door, but I can tell she's faking it. My mom's tears, on the other hand, are real.

My stomach feels full of lead. "What's wrong?" I say.

"There were protest materials at school, and you didn't tell me?"

"No. I mean, yes, I mean, I don't know." I see my backpack, wide open, is lying on a chair. My mom grabs a handful of protest request forms. She stares at me.

"I had some questions," I say.

"Vince Flakeman was at your school? He found protest materials in Hannah Cossack's backpack?"

"I guess so."

"You guess so? Do you guess that Hannah Cossack sends you answers to your math assignments?"

I want to say, *"Why do you believe Jade and not me?"* I want to say, *"When I have questions and need help, no one cares."* I want to say, *"I'm thirteen and I don't know what to do, and I don't have friends anymore."* But my brain is overloaded, and nothing comes out.

"You are associating with someone named Kyle Foster. Who is he?"

I would answer, but I don't know what the right answer is.

"If Flakeman labels him a terrorist, do you know what that means?"

"A *terrorist*? Mom, I don't think—"

"The consequences?" she shouts. "I begged you to tell me about any troublemakers," she says. "Don't you get it? My... your...*our* future...our lives could be ruined!"

This is some kind of mix-up. I want to explain, but I don't know what to explain.

"Don't talk to this Kyle Foster–ever again," she says. "Don't talk to anyone I don't know."

I feel tears welling up, but I don't know how to defend myself.

"I'm leaving," she says as she grabs her respond-pad. "You don't deserve the Academy."

I think this might be the worse possible thing she can say, but as she slams the door, she says something even worse: "Don't come to the safety office anymore."

I don't try to stop my tears. Why did Jade do something so mean? Why do I pretend she's my friend? Why do I have to be blamed for having questions? Why can't I like the boy I want to like? My mom didn't even say she would come back. I don't know if I'm sobbing because I'm mad or scared or confused or lonely.

Hannah

My sisters agree to leave me alone if I let them stay in my room and color. I go to the kitchen where I can think and make a decision.

At the top of a new page in my journal, I write:

Should I go to the True Democracy meeting?

I draw a line down the middle of the page and make two columns. I can't cheat. The winning column must have at least three good reasons. When I make decisions like this, I always know which column I want to win. This time I don't.

YES	*NO*
Attending is different from joining.	*I'll have to lie to my parents about where I'm going.*
~~*Maria will be there.*~~	
~~*I'll see Jonah.*~~	*It might be dangerous.*
I can find out more about the organization.	

After I cross out Jonah and Maria–not relevant–I have only two reasons in each column.

"Come play our game, Hannah," Emma yells from the other room.

I ignore her and try to concentrate. I think of two more reasons – one for each side.

YES	*NO*
I don't like the citizenship rules.	*My dad wants me to embrace citizenship.*

"Stop, or I'll zap you." It's Lily's voice now.

Are they playing Protector? I can't think of a more revolting imaginary game.

Emma runs into the kitchen.

"Tell her it's not fair," Emma says.

"I'm busy."

"Just tell Lily it's not fair."

"What's not fair?" I ask.

"She's using a real one and not her finger."

I jump off the chair and run into my room.

Lily points the Protector at my heart. "Stop, or I'll zap you," she says.

I feel the blood drain from my face as I fight the urge to scream. I make myself walk in steady, confident steps toward Lily and then I hold out my hand. "I'll play Worldopoly," I offer.

"Yay!" they both yell, and Lily drops the Protector at my feet.

One game for another; they don't understand the difference in the consequences.

I thought I'd locked the Protector securely.

Decision over. If the True Democracy people can help me protect my sisters, I'll listen to what they have to say.

When my mom comes home, I grab a book, put the Protector in my purse, and go to the zoo.

I head right for the monkeys and watch them play. After a while, I sit on the bench nearby and read. I glance at the loose wires that Russell showed me. It's so nice to be alone for a while.

Popsicles taste good but stain your teeth orange and your tongue purple. Hannah, want a ride?

I don't hear the name Hannah much on the Broadcaster. It seems funny.

Rides are good for people named Hannah. My bog. Rides are not good for boys named Hannah. Rides are good for girls named Hannah sitting on benches. Hannah, want a ride?

I don't know whether to laugh now or be petrified. People around me show no reaction to the Broadcaster announcements. I try to stay calm as my eyes scan the area. A horn honks. An old junk of a car is parked at the curb. Jonah gets out, takes his beret off and bows like a chauffeur. I can't see it, but I guarantee he has a smirk on his face. I hesitate but then walk over.

"I live close," I say. "I really don't need a ride."

"I really don't want to drive you home."

"Where then?"

"Take a chance."

I put *Gone with the Wind* in my purse. I know all the wonderful qualities of Ashley, and if I tried, I could convince myself that he is the type of guy I should look for. But, If Kyle can pass out protest flyers and Maria can rip up Governcorp logos, I can get in a car with my version of Rhett.

The car is a wreck and full of junk. Jonah sweeps a backpack and papers onto the floor so I can sit down. Foam bursts from the seat cushions, and the car rattles and shakes as Jonah steps on the gas. It jerks and moans with every shift change. Few citizens have cars, but most of them are disasters like this one. They're not against the law, just expensive to operate because of the taxes and cost of fuel. Our car is owned by my dad's store.

"I left my Fox in the garage," Jonah says, and half smiles at me. This time his smirk makes sense. The Fox brand is the luxury car Governcorp officials drive. I smile back.

"Ice cream?" he asks as he accelerates.

"I don't have any money."

"Me neither, but the guy owes me."

My brain wakes up. What am I doing here? I'm with either a thief or a protester–probably both. I think about getting out at the next light, but we hit all the greens at the intersections, and then we've gone so far that I don't recognize anything. I shift my feet among the trash and pick up a thick book.

"Helicopter pilot manual?" I flip through it and notice high-lighted instructions and detailed notes in the margins. "You're studying this?"

"Everybody needs a hobby," he shrugs.

"Are you buying one soon?"

"After the Fox."

I roll my eyes and try to hide my smile.

I watch the scenery, and with each passing mile, even though I know it's an illusion, I feel a little freer. My mood is light when we pull into a parking lot next to a small ice cream stand. There's a line, but Jonah has me stand off to the side, and he waves to "the guy who owes him" inside. Jonah gets a box out of the trunk, and then the man lets us in the side door while he finishes serving customers. He's forty-ish with a mustache and a paunch that no doubt comes from eating too much of his product. He wears an apron that is so full of stains from ice cream and syrup that it looks like artwork. When the last customer leaves, he turns with bright-eyes to Jonah and gives him a bear hug.

"How many did you bring?" he asks as he grabs the box. Then he looks my way, startled. "Who's this?"

"Hannah, what kind of ice cream do you want?" Jonah says.

I guess that was my formal introduction.

"Bringing people here...jeez." The man shakes his head and puts the box in a closet. He stares at Jonah and then at me. I'm so uncomfortable I grab a menu and pretend to read.

"I'll have the usual," Jonah says with a smile. "Double chocolate ripple banana split with extra fudge and whipped cream. Hold the cherries and nuts. Oh, and a long spoon."

Jonah looks at me, and I figure, why not? "Double cone with strawberry and pistachio, please."

The man mumbles and goes over to the frozen bins. He grabs two frozen lemonade Popsicles, hands them to us, and opens the door.

"Thanks, Frizz," Jonah says and heads for the car. He stops halfway and turns. He holds up the Popsicle in the air as if giving a toast and yells back to the man, "Tomorrow."

I just stand in place and try to decide if this is funny or humiliating.

The man mumbles, "Be careful, kid," and I'm not sure if he's talking to Jonah or me, but I know I want to go home.

We don't talk for most of the drive back. I have questions, but they'll only encourage Jonah's behavior, and although part of me wants to find out more about him—everything about him—the sane part of me wants to forget this whole episode. Tomorrow. Was he referring to the meeting? Why did... Frizz... say, "*Be careful?*" I guess the box is full of things Jonah stole from Governcorp. I don't like them either, but stealing is wrong, and now I almost feel like an accomplice. Would our citizenship be threatened? If he's part of the protest group, I could be in trouble for just being with him.

"Frizz wasn't in a good mood," Jonah says finally. "Parade makes him nervous." He eats the last of his Popsicle, and I can tell he's sincere.

My impulse to scream at him passes. The parade makes me nervous too. "It was nice he gave us something for free," I say.

"How's the repeat of eighth grade going?" he asks with a smirk.

"How do you think it's going?"

"The girl with the questions."

I smile, and we go back to silence. A comfortable silence this time. We drive almost too quickly back to a familiar neighborhood. He stops the car near a park.

"Last one there pushes," he yells as he climbs out of the car and runs to the swings.

"You have on running shoes—no fair!" I shout as he jumps onto a swing way ahead of me.

I grab the swing next to him, and after a minute, we go back and forth in tandem.

"You do this often?" I tease.

"I do, actually," he says.

"You do?"

"Motion plays with your brain. I get good ideas here."

"I can understand that," I say. "I walk. To the zoo mostly."

"You talk to the animals?"

"Just the monkeys," I say.

"Excellent choice," he says and smiles at me.

I blush. Does he know I've heard the term?

We swing in silence for a while, and I watch two little girls playing on the slide.

"I have two sisters. You?"

"No sisters."

"My sisters are about that age," I say, watching the girls.

"They bug you much?" Jonah asks.

"All the time."

We smile at each other.

"My brother bugged me."

"He's older now?" I ask.

"No," he says flatly.

I can't read his expression. Sadness? Anger? I start to ask another question, but he jumps off his swing and grabs mine.

"How 'bout some spinners?"

"No," I yell.

"Round and round she goes, where she'll end up, nobody knows," he says it just like a carnival worker.

I scream with laughter and dizziness. When I slow down, I take a deep breath and sigh. Where will I end up?

"Deep thoughts?" he says. "I told you motion has effects."

"I might go to…" I stop myself and look at the poles nearby.

"I broke it last week," he says. "They can't keep up with the repairs anymore."

My dad's voice of warning goes through my head again. I'm thinking of going to a meeting where everyone is like Jonah? Breaking viewers is probably the least illegal thing they do. I'll end up in jail…or worse… and my whole family will suffer.

"I better leave."

"You don't feel safe because the viewer is broken?"

"I didn't say I don't feel safe."

"You didn't say anything–you stopped midsentence."

"You break a lot of laws."

"I don't care about the laws."

"But what if something you do causes a person to get hurt? Someone in your family?"

"People get hurt regardless."

"Your brother?"

He shakes his head and looks at me with a long, pained expression. "You have to learn, there are some questions you don't ask."

He walks away. He picks up a small rock and tosses it over the fence. He tosses another and another while the Broadcaster plays.

I like the new lentil burgers at Donald's. What are they made of? **Official report: The web-jurors for the Christopher Fellow trial have been selected.**

I glance up to see the people selected: an old lady knitting, a man playing pool, a mom at the park, a janitor, a woman who's using a respond-pad. Governcorp has made jury duty effortless. Jurors can do anything they want while they listen to lawyers via their ear-muffs. Then they vote electronically. Doesn't interrupt anything.

Watch channel 2000 to see justice in action. Schools will be closed on parade day.

Jonah sneers at the Broadcaster and then walks to the monkey bars.

I decide the best thing to do is to finish my earlier sentence. "What I was going to say is, I might come to the meeting."

"Come or don't come," he says. "It's a personal decision."

"I know it's a personal decision."

"Okay, then."

He climbs inside the dome structure as if he's in jail.

"I'm not that much different than anyone else," he says.

My racing heart will never believe that.

"I may just want it more."

I walk over and sit on the edge of the monkey bars. "Want it?" I ask.

"Protectors banned. Immigrants able to live anywhere they want and apply for citizenship like it used to be. Unbiased reports on the Broadcaster. Trials with a jury–not something that mocks justice."

He climbs up through the structure, using only one arm and one leg. I watch with one hand over my eyes, sure that he'll fall. But he reaches the top and climbs to the outside, free.

"Life," Jonah says. "I just want it more."

The little girls scream and laugh as they play tag. The morning events replay in my head, and I blurt out, "My sisters played with my Protector today."

Like black magic, saying it out loud makes me relive the terror, and this time I don't have to pretend that having a little girl hold a Protector or having it pointed at me is just a joke. There's a lump in my throat, but I don't swallow it back. I don't care if he sees me cry. He climbs down beside me, and that just makes my tears come faster.

"Hey." He sits down and puts his arm around my shoulder. "They okay? Your sisters?"

I nod.

We just sit for a long time until I'm calm again.

"Sorry," I say.

"That's why risk is nothing," he says.

"What do you mean?"

"I'll take you home."

As he drives, I want to ask him to explain more. I want to ask him more about his brother. I glance at his hands firm on the wheel and the well-defined muscles in his arms. He glances my way, and I'm quick to look out the window before he sees my blush. I see a man on the sidewalk wearing the black-and-white monkey shirt.

"Who designed the hidden monkey shirts? What do they mean, anyway?"

"Huh?"

"We just passed one. I have one too."

"What? Where did you get it?" Jonah says this like it's something I stole.

The master lawbreaker is accusing me?

"None of your business."

"Get rid of it." The tone of his voice is alarming. I shouldn't be with him.

"Stop here," I say. "I want to walk the rest of the way."

To my surprise, he pulls over.

"I didn't mean to yell at you." His voice cracks and he shakes his head. "You figured out the shirt design?"

I don't bother to answer.

"It's dangerous to have one," he says. "It might get you arrested…and, well…I don't want you to get hurt."

"Then why do you have one?"

He pulls his brow in and puts his chin on the steering wheel. He stares out the window. His pensive expression–an expression so unlike him–urges me to ask more questions, but I hold back. He finally looks at me like he's trying to make a big decision. "You see…" he begins. I hold his gaze because I realize, despite everything, the decision I want him to make is to kiss me. I think it might happen, and then he turns away. Maybe he doesn't feel the same way I do. I look down.

"I can walk from here. It was fun to swing," I say.

"It happened in a store–the old-fashioned kind where merchandise is everywhere, and you try things on in dressing rooms." His voice is quiet, and he stares straight ahead. "I told him to wait with me while I tried on some pants, but he took off to go look at soccer balls. Seven-year-olds have no patience." Jonah smiles at the memory, but I see the tear hit his cheek. "I was pissed and tried the pants on anyway," he says as he shakes his head. "When I came out, the first thing I saw was the crowd gathered around the sports equipment. Someone was calling for an ambulance. But he was already dead. The woman who shot him was old. She was aiming for some man she thought grabbed her purse."

He takes a deep breath and rolls his head back. "I want life… for him."

I touch his arm, and without hesitating, we kiss each other. His lips press to mine, and I press back, eager to feel them again and again. His hand goes up and down my arm, and I twist so I can press against his chest and put my arms around his neck. He pulls me even closer. His lips are soft and warm and full and wonderful, and now I understand what it means to melt in someone's arms.

BANG.

We both jump from the hard knock on the hood of the car. "Get a room!" yells a kid with a laughing group of teenage boys.

Jonah looks at me with that raised eyebrow smirk again.

"Don't ruin it," I say.

"I don't want to ruin it." He smiles sweetly and kisses me gently again, and then turns away, blushing.

We sit for a minute.

"Hi," he says.

I laugh.

He touches my cheek and smiles.

I wonder, do you kiss because you're in love, or are you in love because you kiss? I lean toward him and do it again. I'll take either answer.

"You're amazing," he says.

I smile. "I need to get home. Thanks for telling me."

"Compliments are my specialty."

"You know that's not what I mean," I say, pretending to be annoyed.

"Yeah, I know." He turns away again. "Things might happen," he says.

"What things?" I ask.

He shrugs.

"Frizz things?" This time I am annoyed. "Okay, I understand about your brother and that you're willing to take risks." I look in the backseat. The car has a pile of protest forms under a sweat-shirt, and a box of who-knows-what pushed against the window. Monkey shirts? "But, I don't get it," I say. "You're an advertise-ment for everything illegal."

I pick up the backpack that sits by my feet and look inside.

"Ohh," I gasp and throw it back on the floor. Several Protec-tors fall out.

"They're fakes," he says. "I get them for people who can't get permits or who are afraid...of accidents."

I pick one up. It looks real to me. The penalty for selling fakes is terrible. "Feigning allegiance to the country," it's called, and sellers are sent for long prison terms or deported.

"How is this helping? Do you want to be sent to prison?"

He ponders, as if this is a complicated question. He starts to answer then rubs his fingers through his hair. He shifts his body, and he remarks in a lighthearted way, "Nope. I think going for treatment at the Comfort Center would be a lot more fun."

"Never joke about the Comfort Center," I say with my jaw tightened. My mind whirls through the faces of the innocent people the Comfort Center destroyed. People I liked. People who went crazy for no reason. People who disappeared.

As I turn to tell Jonah more, he says in a firm, controlled voice, "Don't move." The tension in his voice sends chills up my spine. I keep my body straight but let my eyes roam to his face. His eyes are glued to the rear-view mirror, and his cheeks are drained of color.

I swallow. "What is it?" I ask in a whisper.

"Shove the helicopter book under the seat, then get out slowly and cross the street with that crowd. Don't look back."

"But…?"

"I'm good."

"But…?"

"Hannah, NOW!"

I stuff the book under the seat, open the door, and get out. My heart thumps against my chest, and it takes all my willpower to walk at a normal pace, cross the street, and not look at Jonah. Once in the crowd, I sneak a look down the block to find out what Jonah saw in the mirror. I gasp when I see a Comfort Center round-up vehicle. Four officials walk in the direction of Jonah's parked car. They must be looking for someone in the area. Jonah should be speeding away, not lingering. I stop in my tracks. He *does* want to be sent to the Comfort Center! Several people push me, and somehow, I move forward. I bite my lip to stop a flood of tears. Why Jonah, why?

When I turn the corner, I'm shaking. I wipe a tear away and reach into my pocket for a tissue. My hand touches the fake Protector. I forgot to leave it in the car! I lean on a building wall to steady myself. I should get rid of it. I must get rid of it. I need to follow the rules. The horrid siren of the Comfort Center officials arresting someone blasts, and I look down surprised to see my hands in fists.

I drop the real Protector in the next trash can and put the fake one in my purse.

Sometimes people need to pretend. Pretend to have control over something. Pretend not to be afraid. Pretend to have a plan or solution. Pretend that the person she longs to kiss again will survive.

Jenny

I don't see my mom all weekend. She comes home when I'm asleep, and she's gone when I get up. But I have a plan to make things right again, and when Monday comes, I'm glad to go to school. At lunchtime, I go to Kyle's locker and wait for him. I need to be professional and not nervous. When he rounds the corner, I stand tall with my shoulders square.

"Jenny?" He smiles at me. "Hi."

"I came to give this back to you." I pull out his protest request form and hand it to him.

"I fill it out wrong?"

"No, it's just all the permits have been given already."

"I don't get it."

"There's only so many allowed, and they've all been given out."

I almost say, "Apply early next year," but even though he used me, I never want him to be a protester. By next year he won't care about this kind of weird stuff anyway. Interests and abilities change with maturity—teachers and the Broadcaster always remind us of that.

"What happened to the other forms?" he asks. "Did any of those people get permits?"

"No," I say. "And if they protest, they'll be arrested."

"The constitution guarantees the right to peacefully protest," he says much louder than he needs to. "It doesn't put a number on it."

"My mother approved fifty people," I say in an equally loud voice. "That's enough."

His eyes flash with anger. "Tell your mother that people will protest with or without permits."

My worry that he just pretended to like me bubbles up. "You were nice to me just so I could get your permits, and now you don't even care about them?" I yell.

"What? I didn't say that!"

"I'm not in charge of permits, but I thought I'd bring yours back to help you. I didn't want you arrested, but now I don't care."

I walk away.

"Jenny, stop."

I turn around because I need to say one more thing. "Jade's father will tell you the same thing about protesters, and I don't think he'll want you to talk to his daughter."

"I don't like Jade!" he yells after me.

"Liar," I mutter as I head for my locker. Hannah's locker is open. Stupid girl can't even shut her door. I throw open my door and scrounge for what I need. Can't the school design lockers so you can find things? I hate this school. I will be so happy to get out and be someplace that matters and have a locker that's not so stupid and no opportunity people and boys who...

"Miss Morgan?"

I jump. Vince Flakeman stands three feet away. I look twice to make sure he's real. He holds a clear plastic bag with a Protector inside.

"Yes," I sputter.

"There's a problem," he says, waving the bag.

"I don't understand."

"Have you seen Miss Cossack's Protector?"

"I helped Hannah get a holder. She brings her Protector now," I say.

"You've been checking?"

I nod, but I can't remember checking in the last couple of days.

"Checking her math and other homework, too?"

I nod, my stomach rolling.

"Quite impressive—your math scores. Interesting that the two of you always get the same answers wrong."

I can feel sweat drip under my arms, and my legs feel plastered in cement. Does he think I cheated or Hannah cheated? Is one worse than the other?

"Must be a coincidence," I say.

"Of course it is." He raises one corner of his mouth, and I think of every villain that ever lived and know Vince Flakeman is just as evil. "What's your excuse for this?"

He takes the Protector out of the bag and tosses it to me.

"That is the Protector Miss Cossack had today when I stopped her in the hall."

It looks different than the prize she won. She got a new one? Why didn't I notice!

"It's fake," he says. "Your Academy application has been denied."

I stare at the Protector.

"Miss Cossack will be taken care of." He grabs the Protector out of my hand and walks out the door.

She can't do this to me! I search her locker. Maybe she has two Protectors. The one Flakeman found is some kind of joke. I look behind her books, her coat, her notebooks–there is no other Protector. Lots of students are in the hallway now. I don't care. I dump books and papers from her locker to the floor. I see two monkey dolls and throw them as hard as I can, but they both skid away without breaking.

The office viewer's speaker comes on.

"Jenny Morgan, report to the office immediately."

I push past the gawkers, pick up the monkeys, and then smash them to the floor again. They refuse to break. Instead, they slide on the floor towards the door. I grab them and run straight for the exit. At home, I'll find a hammer.

I race down the steps and across one street and then another. Several car horns blare at me, but I keep running until my lungs and legs refuse to continue, and then out of breath, I have to stop and bend over with my hands on my knees. My chest burns as I pant.

I don't want to go home. I can't go home. I want to disappear.

When a bus turns the corner and stops, I get on board.

I find an empty window seat and stare out onto the streets without thinking about anything. I hope I get lost. I hope I'm gone for days. I hope the bus crashes. I cling to my backpack like it's a teddy bear. After awhile, I watch people on the sidewalks and choose who I'd rather be. The little girl pushed in a stroller by her dad, a woman with a briefcase going into a bank, a lady walking her dog.

The bus goes by the Homestead. Everything looks so nice. Better than where I live. If Hannah is sent back here, I bet she won't even care. But what have I got to look forward to? My mom isn't even talking to me. I bet Hannah's dad is proud of how pretty she is and how well she can do the math and how smart she is at everything. I wonder how proud Mr. Cossack will be when he finds out Hannah broke the law. I'd like to see his…I'll tell him myself. I get off at the next stop across from the Homestead and walk into the store where I know he works.

The store is smaller than I expected. The aisles are so narrow that regular-size shopping carts would never fit. There are only hand-held baskets by the door. I take one and pretend to shop as I glance around for Mr. Cossack.

The shelves are half empty. There's a small bin with lettuce and apples and potatoes. I don't see any other fruit or vegetables. A sign advertises the mac and cheese I like. The sale price is way more than my mom pays.

Two teenage boys with the H on their shirts wander around.

"Those teenagers are bad news," says a woman as she passes me. "I hate coming here, but it's closer to my house, and my arthritis is bad today."

I nod, wondering why old people tell strangers this kind of stuff.

A door in the back bangs shut, and I see a man carry a carton of canned goods into the store. He's tall and thin like Hannah.

Before I can walk up to him, the woman begins yelling from another aisle.

"You're stealing!" she shouts.

"Nothing to get upset about, Ma'am," responds the man as he puts down the carton and strides towards the woman. I peek around the corner and see that she is pointing her Protector at the teens.

"I saw you stealing," she says to them. "Damn illegals. Give you places to live. Give you schools. But it's never enough."

"I didn't see anything," says the man.

"Go back where you belong," shouts the woman as she waves the Protector.

"I know Marcus," says the man. "There must be some mistake."

"The viewers have the evidence if you don't believe me," the woman says.

"Please," the man says. "Forget this." He lowers his voice and adds, "The boys are hungry. They will pay me back. They're leaving."

"You can't let them get away!" the woman shouts.

BANG!

My heart jumps, and I freeze as the teens whirl past me, knocking down cereal boxes and cans.

BANG! Glass breaks, and boxes crash to the floor.

I crouch down and close my eyes and put my backpack over my head.

BANG! More glass. Pieces fly down my aisle and land near my feet. The boys run out the door.

"I'm shot. I'm shot." The woman sounds hysterical, and I'm too afraid to look. My whole body is shaking.

"You're fine," I hear the man say. "Let me help you."

"I'm shot. I'm shot."

I stand up and pull out my respond-pad to signal for an ambulance.

The man sees me for the first time. "No need to call anyone," he says. He guides the woman down the aisle. "She's upset but fine."

His voice is calm, and he is very gentle with the woman.

"I'm okay?" she clings to his arm as she walks. "The shots. The glass."

"It didn't hurt you," he says softly.

He finds a large box for her to sit on.

"Are you Mr. Cossack?" I ask.

"Yes. Do I know you?" He smiles. "We could not have met. I'd remember your pretty red hair."

I look down the aisle. I can tell the broken glass is from the viewers. Did the woman hit them by accident or did Mr. Cossack hit them on purpose?

His explanation for the teens goes through my head. They were hungry. They'll pay him back. He knows them. I could walk out and forget all this. He seems nice. It's all a mistake.

I look at the viewers again.

"Accidents happen," he says. I see his Protector sticking out from his back pocket.

It *wasn't* an accident. Lies and excuses. Just like Hannah. I use my respond-pad to signal the safety office, and then I pull out my Protector. I'm not breaking any more rules for anybody. "People deserve what they get," I say.

I'm just not sure if I'm talking about Mr. Cossack or Hannah or Kyle or me.

Hannah

My mother is called, and I'm taken to the school conference room to wait. The man and woman inside are calm and polite, and their red-white-and-black uniforms are clean and wrinkle free–sterile.

Mr. Blank smiles sweetly and says I'll have a nice visit at the Center. Everyone has a nice visit.

My mother enters, and when I cling to her, I realize I'm shaking. Ms. Blank offers us tea and cookies. I'm in a bizarre version of *Alice in Wonderland*, and I'm about to go down the blackest rabbit hole there is.

"What is happening?" my mom asks.

"Hannah is not feeling well," Mr. Blank says.

My mother becomes frantic. "She is not sick. She did nothing wrong."

"They found a fake Protector," I say. My voice is no louder than a whisper.

"We are brand-new citizens," my mother says. "How would we know a real Protector from a fake? We don't go around shooting the thing at everyone."

Her voice is strong, and for a second I let myself believe that her argument is persuasive enough to stop this.

"Then I'm sure she'll be home in no time," Mr. Blank explains. "Think of it as a checkup." He smiles.

Ms. Blank says she will scan my family's respond-pads for "problems" and clean them for free–a valuable service. Will they check other things in our house? I put the monkey shirt in a drawer under all my other clothes. What happens if they know what it is? Should I warn my mother or be quiet?

I get close to her ear. "Tell Kyle," I say. "He'll give you advice."

She squeezes my hands so hard they hurt. "Do what they say, Hannah," she says. Mr. Blank takes my elbow, and I gently pull away from my mom's grip.

"You must do what they say," she says blinking away tears.

I nod and kiss her on the cheek.

A black Fox with the official Governcorp flag on the license plates waits at the curb. Mr. Blank escorts me, and I think about others who have been forced into these cars: the ones who scream, the ones who beg, the ones who faint, the ones who are tied up or silenced with a wand. The families suffer forever after watching. I won't do that to my mother. I won't let her feel my terror. I walk with steady steps and look straight ahead.

Mr. Blank, my personal chauffeur, opens the back door for me. I think of Jonah and being in his car and wonder how they can both be real.

The door shuts, and instead of holding back, I let myself sob. Now is the time for this–when I'm alone. Cry for me. Cry for everyone in the Homestead.

The GPS voice in the car announces a traffic pattern change and detours us. I look down the blocked street. A sign stretches over the road:

A Celebration of Homesteads and Citizens

I can see floats lined up and workers installing extra Broadcaster speakers. In just three days, loads of people will line up to claim grandstand seats.

The car turns again. The beautiful iron fence of the Comfort Center comes into view. Tall, stately trees line the perimeter; thick, green grass and blooming roses fill the park-like setting. A dozen Governcorp helicopters rest on the building's roof. The fleet is the only clue to the building's purpose.

I wipe my face with a tissue and blow my nose. I smooth my skirt and push a piece of hair into place.

The car door opens.

I hold my head tall. I'm ready to face what will come.

Jenny

"You shot out the viewers," my mom says to Leo Cossack as she looks at the broken glass in the store.

"Why would I shoot the viewers?" he responds. "The woman…"

"Teenagers stole goods, and you did nothing," my mom interrupts.

"No," he says. "I'm a citizen."

"New citizen. Still on probation."

"No one is hurt," he continues.

"Your daughter apparently is having trouble adjusting to citizenship too. Is she getting her ideas from you?"

"No. What ideas?"

"No more talking," Susan says as she comes in the door. "I'll be your lawyer, Mr. Cossack."

"I have all the evidence needed," my mom says. "The facts will soon be out on the Broadcaster."

"They were kids," Mr. Cossack insists. "Opportunity people don't get enough coupons to last the month."

"Stop discussing this," Susan warns him.

"That's a plain fact," Mr. Cossack continues.

"The fact is you won't be in this country much longer," my mom snaps.

I never thought he would be deported. What will happen to Hannah? Will she be deported too? I thought Vince Flakeman would send the whole family back to the Homestead. I don't understand.

"I'm recommending the Comfort Center for now," my mom says.

"I'm not sick," Mr. Cossack answers.

"We want everyone to be mentally healthy," my mom continues. "I understand your daughter is being treated."

"Treated? What does that mean?" Mr. Cossack asks as he's escorted to a Governcorp vehicle. "I've done nothing wrong."

Hannah's at the Comfort Center?

I'm so confused. Did I do the right thing?

My mom gets in her car without a word. I get in the passenger side without looking at her. She drives too fast and slams on the breaks at a light. I curl up close to the door and stare out the window. My mind replays everything that happened in the store. I didn't know what would happen to Mr. Cossack. What is happening to Hannah? I glance over at my mom.

"I'll put your name in my report," she says with no emotion.

"Oh." I stare at my hands.

"It means you helped find a citizen who broke the law."

I keep my eyes down, but I blurt out. "I thought he would be sent to the Homestead."

"Our job is to find the criminals. Other people decide what happens to them."

Other people like Vince Flakeman. People who don't care. I bring my knees up to my chin and hug my legs. My heart speeds up as my mom turns toward our neighborhood. I don't want to be by myself.

"Can I go back to the office with you? Please?"

My mom looks over at me. There's not even a hint of sparkle in her eyes, and the dark circles seem permanent. She takes a deep breath and lets it out in a huff.

"Why did you ruin your chance at the Academy?" she says.

I feel the tears come.

"I didn't do it on purpose. You're never around to help."

"You know the rules and the laws just as well as I do."

I know she's right, but what happens if the rules don't seem to fit? Should there be another rule that says rules don't count? I'm confusing myself when all I want to do is get back to normal.

"I can help in the office," I say with pleading eyes. "You said "our" job is to find the criminals."

She doesn't say anything but turns right at the next corner— the way back to the safety office. My shoulders relax, but when we drive by the Comfort Center, I get a sinking feeling in my stomach that I don't think will ever go away.

Hannah

The doctor who examines me looks so young she must be right out of school. She's quiet but efficient.

Blood pressure–check.

I wonder: Do we listen to the same music?

Temperature–check. Heart rate–check.

What's your favorite book? Have you ever been to Paris?

Reflexes–check. Breathe in–breathe out. Lungs clear.

Will you ever confess to what you do here? I know the answer to that one. No. To get her Governcorp medical job later, she'll smile and say the Comfort Center was a wonderful experience. She helped so many people.

Eyesight–Okay. Ears and throat, fine. Does she have a dog that loves her no matter what?

"Sorry you haven't been adjusting well to citizenship," she says as she enters my data on her respond-pad. "Can you swallow pills? They're a much easier treatment."

I want to ask, "Much easier than what?" But instead, I just nod.

"Good. Blue and red to start." I put one at a time in my mouth. She hands me a drink and watches me swallow. "I need to check if they went down. Don't want any patients to choke."

She approaches with her little light, and I open my mouth. Unfortunately, they went down.

The nurse leads me to my room. The simple single bed suddenly looks inviting. I rub my eyes, but they seem to close on their own. I lay my head on the pillow. I'm so sleepy...very...very... sleepy.

I hear three or four people enter the room and force my eyes open for just a second. Coats...white coats talking; looking at respond-pads. *Who are your friends?* Don't pinch my arm. I can't move my leg...it's stuck...*Get the strap on the other one.* I need to leave. My leg. Can't move. *Where did the Protector come from?* My arm. Help. So tired. More questions. I put them into my dream. *I'm playing a game with my sisters, then with Maria, then with Jenny. We ask trivia questions. How old are you? Who are your friends? Jonah gets us ice cream. Maria keeps saying we should stop playing, but someone else keeps calling my name. My answers are wrong, and I'm losing the game, and we will have to start again, but I don't want to play anymore. My arm hurts. A black shirt with a monkey tail appears.*

I know whatever is happening is something bad. "Where did it come from?" A man's voice is piercing my ears. My eyes are closed, but I'm spinning on a swing so fast everything is a blur of color. "Who gave you the fake Protector?"

I throw up, and voices yell, and doors slam, and I spin and spin and spin, and then pass out again.

*****

"Everything good?" It's the doctor who gave me the pills earlier. She's visiting my room. How long have I been out? "How's your vision?" she asks.

A violent cramp hits my stomach again, but there's nothing left to throw up. "Sorry," the doctor says. "We want you relaxed and responsive, not sick."

The room spins.

"Drink this," she says. "It helps." A glass is held to my lips, and I take a sip.

It does help.

She has only two heads, not four.

"I'll write new orders," she says as she leaves.

I try to keep my eyes open and focus on a hanging picture. It's an image of a... house? Yes. Good. I sip more of the miracle drink. I try to sit up. I don't keel over. What day is it? It's only today...I mean, I've only been here a day. Or maybe two? I see light from the high window. It's daytime. I slept the night, and now it's day. Is that a rhyme? God. I have to adjust. No, that's not what I mean, not adjust…think...think. I lie down and let my eyes close.

"Hannah." It's the nurse. "The doctor says to drink as much as you can."

She's holding the miracle drink to my lips again. She has one head, but it's spinning. "I brought you a bagel," she says.

"When you feel better, I'll take you to the teen center."

She leaves, and I eat. I'm feeling human again. Was the man asking about the Protector real? My mom's words go through my head: cooperate, do what they say. But what will they do to me next? What if the pills kill me? What if they make me go mad? What if I kill myself?

I wad up bagel pieces into little balls and practice drinking but not swallowing the food. I'm not good at it.

My clothes have been replaced with black pull-on pants with an elastic waistband and a matching black pullover top. Who changed my clothes? When? I can't find my shoes. There are slippers. I run my hand under the edge of the bed, and then I cringe from what I feel. The restraining straps are real. I drink more and try to stay calm. The sound of a helicopter over the building makes me shiver. Is that how the Governcorp interrogates arrive?

The nurse returns and tells me I'm on a new prescription. When she sees I can stand without falling, she gives me a small blue pill. She watches as I put it in my mouth. She hands me the drink. Someone knocks on the door, and as she opens it, I spit the pill into my hand. The orderly at the door wants a signature, but my nurse dismisses her and turns back to me. I adjust my waistband and drop the pill inside my pants. I can only hope it doesn't fall right to the floor.

"Drink," the nurse says. I take a long sip. "I need to check if it went down. Don't want any patients to choke." I'd like to call her

Officer Robot, but refrain. She approaches with her light. I pass. I ask to go to the bathroom. I find the demon pill in my underwear and flush it away.

I'm feeling almost normal as the nurse walks me to the teen center.

"You'll feel relaxed and happy soon. That's our job." She smiles. "All part of the healing process. You'll be ready for counseling and well in no time."

The halls are empty except for a doctor or nurse here and there. A neon sign lights up over an automatic door. *Teen Fun Area.* The nurse punches in a code, and the door opens. I'm in a huge room with games and Broadcasters everywhere. Thirty or more kids my age—all with blank looks on their faces—roam freely. The nurse points to an attendant engrossed in a game on his respond-pad. "Just ask Barney if you need anything."

A girl I've never seen before hugs me. "Please come do collages. You'll be sooo good at it," she giggles. She floats paper around in the air with one hand and ribbon pieces in the other, and dances to music only she hears.

Some kids stare at Broadcaster programs or at their fingernails—either way, the experience seems to be the same. I shiver, and collage girl offers me her shawl. "The reds and blue make purple, and purple is soooo nice. My favorite color."

I'm not sure if she's talking about the pills or the paper, but I sit at her craft table with the other zombies. I watch a boy pour glue on his project until it's covered in a white puddle. He seems pleased with his genius. When he looks up, I gasp. It's Rad. I haven't seen him in weeks—what have they done to him?

When dinner is served, I eat the vegetables and salad–no dressing–I figure these are less likely to be contaminated with drugs. I get my water from the fountain the staff uses. I've spotted two possible exit doors that go straight to the street. I don't let myself think about any repercussions for trying to escape or how I can avoid viewers if I do get out.

All I know is that I'm leaving.

A nurse announces we will watch programs until our medications arrive. I sway and shuffle as I walk, trying to imitate the others. I plant myself in front of a Broadcaster screen close to one of the exits and rack my brain for an idea. The Broadcaster is showing a video of someone making pancakes, but the audio is about the parade. The screen changes to a solar-battery ad with classical music. I need to move in order to think.

I start to get up when a hand firmly pushes down on my shoulder, and a voice whispers in my ear, "Welcome to insanity." I turn to see an older boy, hair sticking out, black shirt too big, and strange glasses. When he turns his head, I recognize him.

"Jonah!?"

"Keep your eyes on the screen. You're a zombie, remember?"

A million questions run through my mind. Is he all right? Has he been drugged or worse? I try to turn again, but he has a firm grip on my shoulder. It doesn't scare me. It makes me feel protected somehow. I keep my eyes trained on the Broadcaster. My heart is pounding. Is it because of Jonah or because of everything else?

"Move your fingers to answer me," he instructs. "One finger means yes. Two means no."

He pauses a second, and then says, "Am I a girl?"

I smile and put out two fingers.

"You passed."

He can still make me laugh.

"You spit out the meds?"

One finger.

"I'll get you out."

"What?" I turn around, and Jonah twitches and jerks and makes crazy noises. It looks like he's in pain. I don't know if I should call a nurse or be impressed with his acting skills. I stare at the Broadcaster again.

"Control yourself," he says.

I stifle a laugh. One finger. I'm so thankful he's here.

"Guy in charge–Gamer Boy? He'll go to the john in fifteen minutes. In eighteen minutes an official will come through the door. I'll deal with him. In twenty minutes Gamer Boy comes out of the john. That leaves you two minutes."

One finger. His subtraction is correct.

"When I move, you go behind the fake tree by the door."

"Hey, you," the official yells to Jonah as he walks toward us.

Jonah squeezes my shoulder and whispers, "You're a natural. You'll know what to do."

Is he kidding?

The official grabs him. "You stay in this area," the official says. He pulls Jonah, now the zombie, away.

I'm afraid to turn my head and watch. Emotion will show all over my face. Fear. Panic. Heartache. Concern.

I close my eyes and remember our conversation in the car. Why did you want to be in this place, Jonah? What mission did you give yourself? Or is it Frizz's doing…something with those monkey shirts? Will you escape with me? Oh, my God. My chest tightens with panic as I realize he didn't finish the instructions!

I watch the clock on the wall. I should at least try to follow the directions—it's better than doing nothing. In fifteen minutes the center official goes into the restroom. Jonah jerks and stumbles to the middle of the room.

He drops marbles out of his pocket and falls to the floor. The noise diverts the viewer to his antics, and I dart behind the tree. My mind drifts to our kiss in the car and how I wish we were back at the park, but I can't let myself think about anything right now except escape. I focus on the door. The alarm light shines bright red over the top. This is impossible. I have no idea what I'm doing.

Sixteen minutes.

Seventeen minutes.

Jonah stands and jerks toward the door.

Eighteen minutes. Nothing has happened.

Eighteen minutes and thirty seconds–a reflection in the glass. Flakeman punches in a code and starts through the door. I squeeze into the corner even more. My knees are knocking, and I can feel my heart thumping so hard it hurts. Jonah is mumbling, "I help,

I help," as Flakeman enters. Jonah knocks into him, sending his briefcase and respond-pad across the room.

The light is green over the door.

Flakeman swears at Jonah.

The door shuts.

That's it?

I was supposed to go out at the same time he was coming in? That was impossible. What is the rest of the plan? Jonah shows no sign of coming my way. I'm on my own. A few days ago, I would not have trusted him, but right now I know he wouldn't give me false hope. Use your brain, I tell myself. Jonah makes another scene as he drops things out of Flakeman's case. Flakeman shakes Jonah a few times and yells. It's clear that everyone's eyes are directed to only one place.

Nineteen minutes, thirty seconds. There's a way. There must be a way.

I give the door one more glance. Still shut. But the light. It's yellow.

I focus all my senses on the door handle, and I inhale like I'm diving to the bottom of the ocean. And then I run.

Jenny

My mom and I go into the safety office. When she tells me Carmichael is out fixing viewers, I sit in his spot, in front of the monitors, without a word. I know I can do a good job. My mom watches for a minute then leaves with her own list of viewers to fix.

I keep my eyes on the screens and flip through the neighborhood viewers faster than Carmichael or even my mom. I press the right keys and code in the broken equipment like the professional I am.

So many are broken. Why are people acting like this?

"Stop the illegal activities." The voice comes into the room from a viewer speaker. How did that happen? I didn't turn the speaker on. I grab the microphone.

"Get away from the viewer," I say.

A pair of fierce eyes fills the screen.

"The right of the people to peaceably assemble shall not be stopped," the voice says.

"Get away from the viewer!" I shout into the microphone.

The eyes move back to reveal an angry, determined face. I can't believe who I see. It's Kyle.

I drop the microphone.

"You hear me in there?" he yells. "I'm a citizen."

He stares right at me. I back the chair away even though my brain knows he can't see me.

"Leo Cossack is a citizen. Hannah Cossack is a citizen. I will protest the arrest of innocent people."

Kyle is gone as fast as he appeared. I stare at the screen, unable to move. Images come and go, but my brain seems dead. It's like I'm watching a foreign cartoon show I can't understand. The microphone buzz finally gets to me, and I make myself pick it up and turn it off.

What is Kyle doing? Should I look for him with the viewers and then talk to him? Before I decide, Carmichael rushes in.

"I'm in the semifinals!" he shouts. He holds his hand up and we high-five.

"You don't look so good."

"I'm okay," I say and look at the monitors to hide my face.

"Look at you," he teases. "Miss Professional."

I shrug, and after he gets coffee, he sits down and works.

"You got a good spot on the float?" he asks after a minute. "The prizes are great this year. Wave and smile to the judges and who knows? The 3200 Broadcaster model might be yours."

He gives me a thumbs-up, and I give him one back. He talks about the card contest and the parade and sports and tech equipment. I just nod every once in awhile to keep him content. My mind is on Kyle. Where is he? I need to convince him that protesting is crazy.

"Do you think it's a good idea to do an active search?" I ask Carmichael. "Look for potential problems?"

"I'm not gonna squeal on you if you play with the cameras," he laughs.

"Thanks," I say.

I search the area where I last saw Kyle, and then I search nearby blocks.

There are too many broken viewers to see much more than treetops, people's shoes, and black. Lots of black.

When I hear arguing voices behind me, I stop my search. Susan and my mom scream at each other as they enter the office.

"Free him," Susan demands. "Leo Cossack has done nothing."

"You know I won't do that," my mom says. "The woman who saw the crime is a reliable citizen. Your client allowed people to steal from the store and then he shot out the viewers to cover up the crime."

"Come on, Emily."

"One of the thieves confessed," my mom explains. "His family apparently...has some needs."

"That you can conveniently help with." Susan shakes her head and walks away.

I wish I could ask what she means.

No one says anything for a long time, and then Susan turns toward my mom. Her eyes are piercing, and I can see the vein in her neck. "My client had the decency to protect human life," she says.

"Stopping a criminal protects the lives of others," my mom answers. "I protect lives of the law-abiding community."

"How about the girl?" Susan asks. "Why did you agree to that?"

My mom finds a storage box and pulls out a protest form along with Hannah's fake Protector. She plays a recording from a viewer that shows Hannah throwing something into a trash can. "We've also learned a group of the protesters call themselves monkeys," my mom says. She pulls up an old message to the Broadcaster.

I applaud the monkeys who have gained freedom. One day it will be me.

Susan takes the Protector and slams it on the desk. Pieces spray everywhere.

"Hey," Carmichael jumps up from his chair but my mom waves him off, and he sits back down.

"You may roll over for Flakeman," Susan continues, "but I won't."

"Are you finished?" my mom asks with her eyebrows raised. Susan takes a breath and then steps back from my mom. "I'll offer your client a deal," my mom says. She uses a quiet, soft voice. The one she brings out when I don't want to eat vegetables or when I want to give up piano or when I ask why my room can't be messy if I like it that way. It's the voice that convinces me the thing she wants me to do is the right thing and not a big deal to give into. I wish I had used that voice with Kyle and Hannah.

"Have Leo Cossack denounce his actions on the Broadcaster in an official report," she says. "I'll repeat it 'round the clock until after the parade. I need to show people who are thinking of causing trouble that they will be prosecuted. Then I'll try to get the girl out. They'll go back to the Homestead for several months but won't be deported. You'll be doing some good. Everyone at the parade will be safer."

"That's bullshit," Susan says.

Official report: Only criminals tamper with viewers.
Come protest the arrest of citizen Leo Cossack on parade day. Signs available at Frey, Mitchell, and Smith, Attorneys at Law.

My mom stares at the Broadcaster. "What the hell did you do?"

Susan stares back at her. "I decided to play the game, too."

"This isn't some classroom exercise," my mom says. "You rile up a crowd on purpose, and anything can happen."

"That's right," Susan says. "Protesters may help free an innocent person."

I'm confused. My mom came up with a way to help Leo and Hannah, but Susan doesn't like it. She wants illegal protesters to show up at the parade?

"I'll take this to the High Court," Susan says.

"Ever consider asking your client what he wants?"

"I know what's best for him."

"Get out," my mom says.

I'm proud of the way my mom has performed her duties, and I want Susan to leave. Instead, she turns and speaks to me.

"Your mother and I used to be on the same side," she says. "You won't remember, but she used to have me sing you to sleep." Her lips form a little smile as she shakes her head.

I glance at my mom. Can't they stop fighting?

"You're about the same age as Hannah," Susan continues.

"Leave my daughter out of your schemes."

Susan moves closer to me. "Do you want Hannah drugged and locked up?"

I turn to my mom. "Drugged?"

"Never mind, Jenny," my mom answers.

"I don't understand," I plead.

Susan reaches out and touches my arm. "Are you her friend?"

"No, she's not her friend," my mom shouts as she steps between Susan and me. Her eyes shoot daggers at Susan. "Carmichael will escort you out," she says. "Think about what you're doing."

Susan glares back. "I was going to say the same to you."

Carmichael grabs Susan's arm, and she gives me one last look as she goes out the door.

My head hurts. I've got to figure this out. The Broadcaster comes on and talks about flowers in a garden and laws protect citizens, and black cars get dirty. I can't think with all the noise.

Then there's a new report.

Official report: New citizen Leo Cossack arrested for not stopping a crime. Follow the law, or you will be arrested. *Protest the arrest of citizen Leo Cossack on parade day.*

My mom goes back to monitoring viewers, but I need to know more.

"Why does Hannah need drugs? Where is she?"

"Medicine. She needs medicine."

"Is she sick?"

"She's being treated."

"For what?" I rack my brain thinking of a time Hannah looked sick. Never.

"What's wrong with her? Can I see her?"

"No. And if you're not going to help here, you can leave."

I stare at the viewer monitors. Hannah's dad got arrested—because of me—and now she's sick? That doesn't make sense.

"Why does Hannah need drugs?" I ask again.

"I told you. She's fine in the Comfort Center."

"You didn't tell me that at all. When did she go to the Comfort Center?"

Who's telling the truth—my mom or Susan? "Did Susan sing to me when I was a baby?"

"I don't know."

"Why would she say that then? Why don't you like her anymore?"

"Jenny, stop asking questions. I need to work."

I stand up and shove the chair away. "You never tell me anything!" My stomach is twisting, but I need to know more. "Why is Hannah in the Comfort Center? What happens there?"

"I'll tell you this," my mom says with tight lips. "Hannah Cossack is of no concern to you. She is no longer your buddy. That's what you wanted all along."

I feel my chest cave, and I bite my lip as I turn away and stare at the desk. I kick the chair back and slump into it. What my mom says is true.

Official report: Families of traitors will be deported. Good Citizens are proud to use Protectors. *I don't know the words to the songs that birds sing. The parade has eighty-three floats, five bands, and two cadet teams marching. Comfort Centers are quiet and soothing and help opportunity people. Thank you, Miracle Fill Pharmacy, for your support of our dear clients.*

"That's crap!" a voice yells behind me.

The shout hits my ears at the same time I hear the door slam against the wall as it's thrown open. A second later Kyle stands in the room, and my mom has her Protector aimed at his head.

"Hands up. NOW!" she shouts.

"Stop watching us on the viewers!" Kyle says. He slowly raises his arms and then notices me. "So, you're here." The vein in his neck bulges as he stares me down. "Watching...or is it programming...viewers?"

I feel the heat rise to my cheeks. I don't know if I'm embarrassed because I'm face to face with Kyle or because I am here. Here in the safety office where I thought I belonged.

"Are you a citizen?" My mom's in-charge voice again. "Answer."

"I know my rights."

"You have no right to be in this office. Where's your Protector?"

"Gun," Kyle corrects.

"Where is it?"

"Protectors are weapons, and Speedy Passes are filed fingerprints, and Personalized Coupons and Instee Orders are tracking devices. Comfort Centers are prisons that brainwash people, and Homesteads are ghettos to keep people paying for what Governcorp wants."

"I'm not asking again." My mom's icy tone makes me shiver.

"Mom?" I whisper.

I want to tell her that now I know the answer to her question from ages ago. This is Kyle. I don't know if he's done anything wrong, but he's nice and makes me laugh. He's the boy I wish would hold my hand. The boy who has a nice smile. And even if I don't understand why he does things, he believes in the things he does–just like you, Mom. He's a boy I had lunch with and would have told you about if you made time to listen instead of always working for Governcorp. He's the boy who likes me.

"Mom?" I try again.

Her body, head to toe, appears tensed, focused only on the intruder.

Kyle raises his chin and speaks with a steady voice. "Hundreds, maybe thousands, will protest the laws at the parade. You can't stop them."

He reaches into his pocket, and the unspeakable happens.

Officer Emily Morgan shoots him in the leg.

I can't move. I can't even scream. I stare at Kyle's white face and watch the red stream flow down his pants. He stumbles to the floor, moaning as his eyes close.

"Get his Protector. Out of that pocket."

This is another horrible movie. It's a scene from a blockbuster where the bad guys get mixed up with the good guys. The good guy fumbles into the wrong place and things go wrong. The world is in slow motion. I look at Kyle. I look at my mom. Hours go by. My mom walks over to Kyle and reaches into his pocket. She pulls out a protester request form. Ambulance sirens get closer, and I feel my shoulders being pushed until I'm plopped into a chair. The Broadcaster tells more stories about cars that have wheels or fly, and birds that swim or get shot, and when the shrill warning wails, I cover my ears, but it does no good.

This is a message from the Emergency Broadcasting System. This is not a test. A person has been discovered missing from the Middletown Comfort and Health Center. Anyone knowing the whereabouts of this girl must call the nearest Safety Office.

I look up, but I already know what I'll see. Hannah's face flashes over and over.

This girl needs medication and may be dangerous. Use your Protectors. Her name is Hannah Cossack.

I don't understand anything.

Hannah

I'm thankful for the Comfort Center's black clothes as I race down the block as fast as the stupid slippers will allow. I keep moving and try to remember the parts of the neighborhood with the fewest viewers. I wish I had paid more attention when Kyle told me about ones that are broken. I can't go back to my house. I can't go back to the Homestead and get someone else in trouble for hiding me. Where?

A person has been discovered missing from the Middle-town Comfort and Health Center. Anyone knowing the whereabouts of this girl must call the nearest Safety Office.

I duck behind some bushes and watch my face flash bright and clear on the screen nearby. It's worse than I could have imagined.

This girl needs medication and may be dangerous. Use your Protector. Her name is Hannah Cossack.

Think!
The True Democracy meeting place?
I hear the Broadcaster announcement more times than I can count as I run to Flag street. Which building is it? All of them are old and dark and look abandoned. There's no sign of people. Maybe I can kick out a window and hide inside somewhere. I

walk to the back of the closest building, scanning for a low window, and then someone grabs me around the chest from behind.

"You're trespassing!" a man's voice booms.

He turns me around and flashes a light in my eyes. I bring my free arm up to shield my eyes, but the light is blinding. I squint and look away from the light as much as possible, but he keeps it trained on my face. Without a clear target to see, I kick into what I hope is a groin. I hit a knee.

"Shit," he yells and grips my arm with such force I feel the bruise start. I try again and hit a leg, but he pulls my arm behind my back and pushes me toward the building without even breathing hard.

Inside he shuts the door and turns on a dim overhead light. His tattoos cover all visible skin, and his muscles bulge. He wears a gold earring in both ears, and his head is shaved on one side. The Protector in the holster on his belt might be the least scary thing about him.

"Fool," the pirate man mumbles as he draws his lips into a snarl.

He points me toward the steps. I hear voices as I descend the stairs, and when I get to the bottom, I see people packed shoulder to shoulder in the small room. They face a blackboard where a woman draws arrows and diagrams on a map of the city. The man pulls me through the crowd and row by row, people turn and whisper.

"Hey," the woman says. "Quiet, huh?" The woman has beautiful premature silver hair down to her shoulders. Her features are sharp, and even though she's petite in height and stature, she comes across as someone others don't ignore. The man is still holding my arm as we reach the front.

"Come on, people." The woman slaps her fist on the board and turns. She stares right into my face. The room is silent for what seems like forever. Her mouth curves into a slight smile. "Wow," she says. "Plans have just changed."

Some of the people yell "No!" and others cheer. At the uproar, the man lets go of my arm, and then walks to the front and holds his right arm in the air for all to see. A fist. "Our purpose," he says in a booming voice. The crowd quiets, and everyone holds a fist up too. What is this group? It can't be the one Kyle joined.

The man comes toward me and sneers.

"Wolf," the woman says to him. "A chair?"

Wolf? I've never met a person so befitting his name.

I sit next to the woman. "Welcome, Hannah," she says. "I'm Melanie."

"How did you know...?"

"Let's just say anyone in the city who doesn't know your name by now is blind or deaf." She turns to a lady nearby. "Get the child some tea." The lady walks into the next room without hesitation. Melanie gives orders, and people follow.

"I think you can help us," Melanie says with a smile.

"We don't trust strangers," Wolf says to her. "She knows nothing of us."

I feel insulted because I can be trusted—in normal life. On the other hand, I don't like it that these people assume I want to be involved with them at all, and Wolf hasn't exactly been nice. Who are they anyway?

The woman brings tea, and Melanie and Wolf move to the side and talk in private. The room is buzzing with animated conversations and arguments. I hear snippets of discussions from people near me. "What can she do?" "It's too dangerous." "The original plan was fine."

I'm bursting with questions about this group. What do they believe in? Do they know about Kyle's group? When Melanie turns my way, I ask, "Do you—?"

"In a minute," she interrupts. She's only interested in her conversation with Wolf. A conversation I can't hear.

The crowd hisses and swears at the Broadcaster as it gives more reports. It's odd to hear so many people openly express their hate for the Broadcaster. There are people of all ages and types: citizens who wear suits, others in factory uniforms, teenagers, opportunity people who have holes in their shirts where the H should be, a few doctors or nurses in scrubs. I even see a group in Governcorp jackets. A group of guys in jeans arguing in the corner makes me think of Jonah.

I walk over to Melanie and try again. "Do you know Jonah?"

"What do you know about Jonah?" Wolf barks at me.

"He helped you escape?" Melanie asks.

I nod.

"Don't be angry with her, Wolf." Melanie looks at me and says, "He has a mind of his own."

I'm not sure if she means Jonah or Wolf.

"He needs to be better controlled. Operating like this," Wolf says.

"Getting her out will work for us," the woman says. "You know true rebels are most effective. Not like that peace group."

"Are you talking about—?" They walk away before I can finish the sentence. So, this is a different protest group. How many groups are there? I look closer at the crowd and notice many people have Protectors and no one has on a monkey shirt.

Official Report: Leo Cossack arrested for not stopping a crime.

I cough and spill my tea. Melanie brings me a napkin.

"You didn't know?" she asks.

I shake my head.

"Probably happened while you were in the Comfort Center."

"Is he okay? Do you know where he is?" I ask.

"They say he shot out viewers in his store and let some teens steal food," she says flatly. I can't tell if she thinks this is right or wrong.

"People are hungry," I say. My mind goes to something I always avoid. There was a horrible time in the grocery store when I saw someone shot by a Protector. I'm glad my dad couldn't do it.

"Do you believe he's innocent?" Melanie asks.

"He's not guilty of a crime," I say.

She grabs my hand and squeezes it. "You can proclaim his innocence to the entire community at the parade."

"That's not our purpose," Wolf says under his breath.

"We need a distraction," Melanie mumbles back.

"We have the float."

"What are you talking about?" I ask.

"People will like your story," Melanie continues, ignoring my question. "The pretty girl drugged unfairly, and her father only trying to help hungry people. Their eyes will be glued to you as you lead a group of protesters into the parade."

"I can't lead protesters," I say.

"You would be a wonderful leader. Besides, you don't want to go back to the Comfort Center or have your family deported, do you?"

"No. Of course not."

"Then we'll help you tell people your father is innocent."

Her voice mesmerizes. She widens her eyes and draws me in. Be a believer, her face beckons. Yet there's something…the corner of her mouth that angles up just a little too much on one side?

"After it's all over," she continues, "we'll be glad to provide you with something." The voice reminds me of someone. "We have resources." She flashes a fake smile. Why not just say, "You scratch my back, I'll scratch yours." At least animals do it out of affection and love.

"The timing has to be perfect," Wolf says to Melanie.

"Shh. Later," she says. Then she turns to me. "You'll need a good night's sleep. Sunshine in the morning."

I gasp. "You're the voice of the Broadcaster!"

She raises her eyebrows and that same corner of her mouth. "Am I?" Then without missing a beat, she takes my elbow and guides me away. "I'll find you a nice room," she says.

I let her lead me, but my instincts tell me to run. She hasn't given me a direct answer to any of my questions and is planning something with Wolf she doesn't want to tell me about. And if she is the voice of the Broadcaster, she works for Governcorp. How can I trust someone I don't understand? I just want my dad safe. This woman doesn't care about him or me. I wonder what he's doing right now. Is he being drugged? Tortured? Would he cooperate with these people?

Melanie shows me to a room on the first floor. It smells of dirt and mold. There is a large window covered with newspaper. Old office furniture is pushed into a corner, and there are three cots in the middle of the room. She points to the one with a blanket and pillow and tells me goodnight. I know I need to move as fast as possible. When I hear her fading footsteps, I quietly pull the newspaper off the window. I look out and confirm that the ground is within jumping distance. I wiggle the old window up an inch at a time until I can squeeze through.

I need to be someplace I understand and where I feel safe. I'm going to the zoo.

Jenny

I wake up at noon–alone. The sleeping pill my mom gave me worked as she said, and I didn't have any nightmares. Who needs a nightmare in your sleep when you can have one wide-awake? I want to stay in bed and forget everything, but instead, my mind makes me remember all the details.

Blood. Ambulance. Noise. Blood. Kyle. Hannah. Blood.

Stop thinking, I tell myself. But my mind is still racing.

Kyle shouldn't have come into the safety office. He shouldn't have yelled into the viewers. He shouldn't be protesting. My mom had no choice but to follow the law when she thought he was going to pull out his Protector.

Hannah should have followed the rules. The Comfort Center was helping her.

My stomach knots. If I would have told my mom I knew Kyle, she never would have shot him. He wouldn't be in the hospital and under arrest now. I just stood there. I didn't know blood would be so…so…everywhere. Forget. Just forget.

I need to be someone to be proud of. I pull up Math Tutor and read the directions for problem four. Any dummy can do problem four if they try hard enough. Any dummy who wants to pass. I do the problem over and over until my respond-pad says "correct."

Is Kyle lying in the hospital thinking how much he hates me?

Don't think about yesterday. I can't think about yesterday.

The Broadcaster buzzes. It's my mom on the screen.

I stand up straight.

"You're okay?" she asks.

I nod and look straight into her eyes. Why wouldn't I be okay? I'm a professional. I need to tell my mom I'll do better. I will be more serious and follow the rules as I should.

"Mom, I..."

"It wasn't your fault. I put Carmichael on probation for never locking the door properly," she says. "It's important to put this behind you."

I nod.

"The best thing to do is take action. Never run from it. Come to the office, and I'll have a job for you."

When I enter the safety office, only Carmichael is there. I don't want to, but I look at the spot where Kyle fell. It seems like it happened years ago. It seems like it happened seconds ago. Put it behind me. Put it behind me.

Carmichael's Protector sits in front of the monitors, and before I sit down, I move it closer to him. He stammers an apology and says he would never put me at risk on purpose. I don't know what to say, so I ask him to show me another card trick. He shuffles the cards and then pulls four aces from behind my ear.

"How do you make the cards do that?"

"The hand is faster than the eye," he says. "A good magician can make people believe anything."

My mom enters, and Carmichael scrambles to hide his cards, but my mom doesn't even look his way. She walks to her desk with a blank look on her face, slumps into her chair, and stares at a screen. Finally, she says, "Comfort Center personnel are morons. They have no idea how Hannah Cossack left the facility. Have you seen any signs of her?"

Carmichael shakes his head no.

"Jenny, any ideas?" I shake my head no, too. I sit up straight and review more streets. Carmichael and I determine that two hundred viewers in critical areas are not working. Hundreds more around the city are broken too, but my mom says we can't worry about those now.

Carmichael whistles–who-eee–like a cowboy from an old show. "Sounds like we need National backup," he says. He pretends to ride a horse, and I laugh until I look at my mom. She blinks away tears, then in one swift motion she grabs Carmichael by the collar and leans into his face.

"I will not show incompetence," she says emphasizing each word. "That's what they all want from me–your uncle, Susan, National–the whole damn world."

She lets go of Carmichael and paces.

"This parade is going to work, Carmichael," she says. "Other cities may shut down; other cities may call for backup; other cities may have riots. But we will be the shining example for Governcorp. Do you understand?" She walks over to Carmichael again. He's practically cowering in his seat, shrinking down as low as he can. Even I think she might hit him. "Are you resigning or are you doing the job?" Unblinking, she stares into his face.

Carmichael doesn't answer; he swallows hard, then downloads all the data about damaged viewers.

Another Broadcaster announcement comes on about Hannah. It talks about her all the time now. Few people just walk out the door of the Comfort Center.

My mom sighs and leans on the desk. "I can't protect that girl," she mumbles. She closes her eyes. I watch for a minute and then gently touch her shoulder.

"Should I make coffee?" I ask.

She lifts her head and nods, and in a too-quiet voice says, "Please."

As I measure the coffee and water, I rack my brain to think of a way to convince her to help Kyle and Hannah. Before I think of anything, I hear her screen-call with a Comfort Center official. Maybe they found Hannah or she went back. I crack open the break-room door and listen.

"Bridgett, I need information on case 8779," my mom is saying. "That kid who came in the safety office."

She's finding out about Kyle.

The woman on the screen looks up some information and then says, "Hospital reports fair condition."

Is "fair condition" hospital-speak for good or bad?

"He's cooperating?" my mom asks.

"Not sure," the woman responds.

My mom's beeper activates. "Hold on, Bridgett." She turns away from the screen and answers the call from Vince Flakeman.

"Morgan," she barks in her most authoritative voice.

"Do you understand our situation?" Flakeman's voice is so loud it sounds like he's in the room.

"I'm aware of the situation," my mom replies in a steady voice.

"Get those protesters under control! Half of them are teenagers. That kid you've got is a leader. Use him."

"No."

"Use him!" he yells.

"He may not cooperate."

"You know we don't need his cooperation."

"That's overreacting."

"Overreacting would be to fire you now before you've had the chance to prove your own incompetence!" Flakeman yells. "Something happens at that parade, and I lose my move up to National, I guarantee you'll never work again – or worse!"

My mom throws the beeper across the room. Carmichael and I both jump and gape at her. I don't even try to hide the fact that I'm now standing at the break-room door, eavesdropping in full view. My mom looks over at the monitors and watches a few people go by on a street near the parade. After what seems like forever, she goes back and talks to Bridgett. "I'll authorize voice recognition," she says in the softest voice possible.

Voice recognition? That's when a person's words are put on a computer and made into new sentences. Flakeman wants to do this to Kyle?

"Only if needed, Bridgett," my mom continues. "Only if absolutely necessary. Try to get cooperation. I'll send over something that explains how lives will be saved."

I look at Emily Morgan, safety officer. An official, not my mom. I know she is competent and determined but also sad and worn out. Doing what Flakeman wants is wrenching her insides.

"What will he make Kyle say?" I ask. "Kyle's not a terrorist. He's not even a bad person. He's…" I stop because if I say he's the person I like, that might make things worse.

"He's what?"

"He's just a kid in my school who's smart. He didn't do anything wrong."

My mom takes the thermos of coffee from me. "That's not for you to decide." She turns away and points toward her official respond-pad on the desk. "Blast the Broadcaster with the warnings I wrote while Carmichael and I fix viewers."

I shift my weight and press my lips together. "Hannah's not a terrorist, either," I say.

"She's a confused girl who would be much safer under arrest," my mom says as she grabs her tools. "When we finish, I have to drive to Centerville for a cable replacement to keep the extra viewers operational," she continues. "I'll be back before the parade starts."

I want to say more about Kyle and Hannah, but in a flash, my mom is out the door with Carmichael.

I punch in all the codes and start the messages. I turn up the Broadcaster so I can hear everything.

Official report: Protesters without permits will be arrested. *Mosquitos show up in the dark and get you by surprise. Comfort Center girl who escaped is dangerous. I'm getting a monkey for a pet. They're smarter than dogs.*

Monkeys for pets. Monkeys.

My mom's voice comes into my head. "Take action." I grab my Protector and put the respond-pad in my backpack. I know where Hannah Cossack must be hiding. The zoo!

***

I hear tons of Broadcaster messages as I walk to the zoo.

Kyle Foster is a terrorist. Terrorist girl has red hair.

Terrorist girl has red hair? What girl? If the Broadcaster means Hannah, she has blonde hair. And Kyle is not a terrorist.

Protest the arrest of Leo Cossack.
Hannah Cossack must be stopped from committing more terrorist acts.

What does that mean, "terrorist acts"? What did my mom mean when she said, "I can't protect her?" She can't protect terrorists, or she can't protect Hannah if people think she's a terrorist? Is Kyle considered a terrorist because he came through an unlocked door, or because he wanted a protester permit?

My mom says an officer works with facts. Yes or No. True or False. Facts. So why are these facts confusing? I need to stop thinking and send in more official reports. I find a bench at the zoo entrance and sit to enter the codes.

Official report: Boy attacked Middletown Safety Office.

Boy attacked safety office? Did my mom really mean that? Did I key it in wrong? I search the messages and see I entered it correctly. But that's not what happened.

Hannah's face comes up on the Broadcaster near me. Instead of the official Governcorp message, my brain hears her laugh and tell me: "One day you'll believe the things I say." Her voice is so clear in my head, it freaks me out.

Thick air is hard to swallow. If I put too many strawberries in my blender, will it blow up?

"Stop!" I look at the machine and yell as though it might listen.

My dog Max loves his electric fence. The Emperor's New Clothes is a good history story.

"Stop!"

I feel my teeth clench and my muscles tense, and then I jump up from the bench and run. I run past the closed food stands, past the mini train station, past the entrance to the giraffes, past a sign for lions, past the goats, past the reptile house, until finally, I slow down, my lungs and legs aching, as I see the monkeys' caged area.

The shadows hide most of the animals, but I can make out a few asleep in the fake trees. I look around for places Hannah might be hiding. The bushes in a corner seem like the best spot. I stand where I have an unobstructed view to see any movement. I clutch my Protector then take a deep breath. My voice comes out loud and strong.

"I know you're here. Come out."

The noise wakes the monkeys, and they move around and call to each other. There are dozens of them crowded together in the little tree.

She must be here somewhere. I shout louder. "You can't hide from me!"

The monkeys must think I'm yelling at them because they scream horrible sounds. They call each other and scream louder and louder. The shrill shrieks get to me, and I have to put my Protector in my pocket so I can cover my ears with my hands. I move a few feet away, and out of the corner of my eye, I see Hannah sneak out from behind a bush to escape. I rush toward her and grab the Protector from my pocket. I point it at her heart, and she stops. The monkeys screech even louder.

"Make the monkeys stop!" I yell.

"I don't know how."

"Yes, you do!" I holler.

"We have to be quiet," she says.

My head pounds with the continuous shrieking and I bite my lip to keep from screaming myself. Hannah's eyes dart to the path, and I step closer holding the Protector steady to make sure she doesn't run.

Hannah

If I run, how far would I get? Jenny stands like a sentry and has the Protector pointed right at me. I look down as I cover my ears with my hands. The noise from the poor, scared monkeys is deafening. Even the Broadcaster nearby can't be heard.

Minutes pass as we stand in silence waiting for the monkeys to settle down. I raise my head and see my picture on the Broadcaster screen. I shiver from head to toe knowing that citizens, like Jenny, are being reminded to use their Protector. The screeching subsides enough for Jenny to give an order.

"I'm taking you to the safety office."

She stands straight with her chin up, looking down her nose at me. How dare she pretend to be righteous? My muscles tense and I speak in a steady voice. "Did your mother send you? Are you an official now?" I ask. My words fuel my courage. "You figured out I had a fake Protector and had me put in that terrible place. I'd throw the real one away again."

Her hand touches the trigger of the Protector, and she inches closer to me. "Shut up," she says. "I'm trying to help you!"

I glance down at the Protector. I should stop talking, play nice, or maybe beg and be humble, but my blood is boiling. "Were you just mad because I refused to ride on a parade float? Don't worry. I'll be at the parade. I'll wave to you up on your precious float when I'm in the street with Kyle and all the other protesters and—"

"STOP it!"

The monkeys give a loud, long screech, and then grow silent again. The Protector is so near, I can see the On/Off button. It points to "On." Without warning, I begin to sweat, and I gasp for breath as the horrible memory takes over my body. The memory of seeing a person shot. The memory of seeing a person killed. I shake my head pretending I can stop the details from flooding my brain. But as I look at Jenny's Protector, my knees tremble, and I'm back at the scene. Charlie is in the store, confused as usual. Governcorp stopped the money for his medicine to treat his psychosis. He was hungry and put some cheese in his pocket, and when a citizen accused him of theft, he said his friends would pay. His invisible friends. My dad tried to explain and offered to pay, but the citizen ignored everything and shot Charlie as soon as he went out the door.

I feel tears drop on my cheek and quickly wipe them away. I look past the Protector and glare at Jenny. "Do you really want to see it?" I say.

"See what?"

"The person looks white suddenly and can't breathe, and his eyes look at you, but you can tell he doesn't really see you standing there."

"What are you talking about?"

"It just looks wet at first. A wet, black spot. And then you see the red stream flowing, and the person falls to the floor, and his eyes turn into his head. And he lays there, and if he's from the Homestead, the ambulance never comes. It's something you NEVER forget."

Jenny's Protector hand shakes, and she steadies it with her other hand then takes a step closer. I step back, trip, and land on the ground. I scoot away, but my back hits a fence. There's no place to go.

Jenny widens her stand. Could she really shoot me? "Do it fast," I say as a curl myself into a ball.

Hannah Cossack is a terrorist. Official Report: Protesters without permits will be taken to the Comfort Center. Kyle

Foster is a terrorist. Smile at the viewers. They take good pictures. No red eyes.

I stay still while more noise blasts from the Broadcaster. Jenny seems too silent, and I glance up, afraid I'll look right into the Protector. Instead, I see Jenny's pained expression and tired eyes looking down at me and tears on her cheek. Her shoulders slump, and if I didn't know her age, I'd think she was a worn out, weary adult. She lets her arm flop down as though the weight of the Protector is finally too much. We both look at the strange thing. I can read the official slogan clearly. *Together We Are Strong.*

Don't take my chair at the parade. Cut up apples have fewer calories. What's better? I'm smart. Your size shoes on sale at Buy Now. My microwave oven burns food. People with red hair are terrorists.

Jenny's nostrils flare, and she opens her eyes wide and glares at the Broadcaster. I jump as she heaves the Protector right at the ugly box and lets out a horrible, sad scream.

"I hate everything" she yells. "Everything."

Jenny

The Broadcaster glass shatters everywhere. My heart pounds against my chest and I struggle to catch a breath. The monkeys screech again. They jump up and down and bare their teeth. Shut up, I think. You're not fierce; you're terrified, just like me. Hannah is saying something, but my brain is tired. My arms are tired. My legs are tired. I let myself collapse to the ground and close my eyes. I'd give anything to wake up in my bed next to my mom.

When the monkeys quiet again, I'm crying and so is Hannah.

"I saw it too," I whisper. "It was Kyle."

Hannah's eyes widen, and she puts her hand over her mouth. "Is he? Is he—?"

"In the hospital. It's his leg. He came into the safety office and my mother…my mother." I choke on the words and my tears. "I stood there. I couldn't stop her," I say. "If I knew how horrible… how horrible…I wouldn't have reported it."

"Reported what?" Hannah asks.

"I was in your dad's store," I say.

She jumps up and backs away from me. "How could you!?"

"I was angry over your Protector. Vince Flakeman is the one who found out and then he told me I couldn't go to the Academy. I went to the store to tell your dad you broke the law. I wanted to get back at you. Your dad was so nice."

"Stop," Hannah says.

"He even said he liked my hair, and I did it anyway." I cover my face as I cry. "I knew he wasn't lying about the boys."

"Stop!" Hannah yells as she walks away.

The adrenaline I had is gone, and I'm exhausted from crying and running and…confessing. I wish the monkeys would scream again because I'd rather hear them than think about everything. I don't even know what side I'm on. I've failed my mom and Hannah.

"I'm sorry," I say. Hannah refuses to look at me. "Please understand," I beg. "I'm just so sorry about so much. I'm all mixed up."

A Broadcaster not too far away blasts another announcement about Hannah. We look into each other's eyes, and she whispers, "We should get out of the open."

We move into the shadows of the bushes and rest our backs on the fence.

She blows her nose and inhales deeply several times. I feel like she's recharging both of us.

"I won't tell anyone you're here," I say. "I'll go."

I look at the black clothes she has on. The Comfort Center clothes.

"You're brave," I say.

"Kyle is brave," she answers. "My dad is brave."

I start to get up, but Hannah pulls me back. "Stay," she says.

"You ran away," I say. "I could never do something like that."

Hannah shrugs. "I wanted to survive and running from the Comfort Center was the easiest way to do it."

"You always know what to do, and I can't figure anything out," I stammer.

Hannah glances at the broken Broadcaster. "You threw away the Protector. You told me the truth."

I think for a minute and then say what I've known for a long time. "You're the only person who has always told me the truth. And I never believed you." I grab the two monkey figurines from my pocket and hand them to her. "From your locker."

Hannah

I take the figurines and let out a sigh at their unwavering simple expressions. I wish I could cover up my eyes and ears and make every problem disappear. Where's my dad? What's happening to Jonah? Are my sisters and Mom okay? What will happen to me?

"I try to follow the rules," Jenny says. "But...some things shouldn't be rules. I think about what I'm supposed to do and what my mom says it means, but it's not what it is." She frowns and grimaces. "I'm not explaining things right. I never explain things right!"

She tugs at pieces of her hair and curls her shoulders over her chest. I almost reach out and touch her arm.

We hear the Broadcaster down the street predicting sunny weather or rain for tomorrow's parade, and telling us we will love a new sweater, and that a certain drug makes you happy all day long.

Jenny shakes her head and covers her ears. "I don't want to go back to things I don't trust." She turns to me with wide eyes. "How do you know what's real?"

The question—so simple—but nothing around us seems to give a clear answer. I hug my knees and feel my chest bottle up. "Maybe it's just what you feel in your heart," I say, thinking about all the people who are in mine.

"I have to tell Kyle I'm sorry," Jenny says. She picks up a figurine and traces the details of each monkey with her finger. "See no evil. Hear no evil. Speak no evil," she says. "You have to remind other people of that, or everyone keeps following the wrong rules." Her face lights up.

I smile and realize Jenny has just explained everything perfectly.

Jenny

In the distance, I hear sirens. Everyone is looking for Hannah. Maybe my mom is looking for me. Maybe others are looking for me, too. I pull out the respond-pad.

"I'm supposed to send official messages to the Broadcaster. This one is about Kyle. The officials want him to ride on a float tomorrow as an example."

"Example of what?" Hannah asks.

I read the message. "Injuries happen when protesters go against Governcorp laws and regulations."

"He'll never agree to that."

"They'll lock him on the float," I say.

"Display him—injury and all? Like an animal?"

I put my head down and say the words I dread. "Your dad, too."

"I have to go back." Hannah jumps up, but I grab her arm before she can go far.

"No," I say.

"I don't care what happens to me anymore. I can't let this happen to my dad."

"Going back might not do anything."

"They want to know how I got a fake Protector."

"You'll turn other people in?"

"I don't know. No. Why can't you ask your mother to stop it all?"

"I could, but she's in Centerville." I don't mention that I'd have to convince her to go against Flakeman's orders.

The Broadcaster down the block sends a message reminding citizens to watch for protesters.

Hannah hears it too and wrinkles her brow. "They don't mean, watch," she says. "And if people consider my dad and Kyle protesters or enemies of Governcorp...?"

Her voice trails off, and I feel a knot in my stomach. "What will the protesters do at the parade?" I ask.

Hannah whispers back, "I don't know."

I watch Hannah look blankly into the distance. I can't stand the idea of her being afraid because if she is, I will be too. I use my best scolding voice. "You were supposed to say, 'what do you think they'll do?'"

We both smile a little, and Hannah finally says, "I guess...I'm afraid of the answer."

Answers. Yes or No. A, B, C, or D? They won't fit. Even copying from someone won't give you the real answer. You must find it for yourself.

I look at Hannah's figurines again. One is just a single monkey. "Who's this?"

"Shizaru. Do no evil," she says. "He's the most powerful."

I study him for a minute and say, "He must be the bravest."

Hannah nods.

"Can I keep him?" I ask. "Just for awhile?"

Hannah nods again. I push all the negative thoughts away and all the 'what-ifs' that could happen, and put Shizaru snugly in my pocket.

"Let's go," I say. "We have to keep Kyle and your dad off the float."

***

At my house, I give Hannah clothes and shoes, and we both put our hair up under hats and wear sunglasses that hide our faces. I find the official respond-pad and type in new messages: ***Hannah Cossack is not a terrorist. Leave your Protectors at home. Kyle Foster is not a criminal. Protectors kill. Leo Cos-***

sack is not a criminal. The Broadcaster lies. I wait until I hear them play as official reports on the Broadcaster and then I shove the respond-pad under my bed.

"You're not bringing it?" Hannah asks.

"If the tracers come back on, my mom will know where I am, and she won't understand until I explain," I say. Vince Flakeman will know where I am too, I think, but I don't say it out loud.

It's dawn, and the Broadcaster has already announced crowds are beginning to form. We walk towards the parade.

I remember where some of the broken viewers are and lead Hannah down those streets. Broadcasters blast parade music and messages from the crowd. We hear my messages off and on, but much too often, the information about Hannah, along with her picture, flashes for all to see.

We pass beer and brat stands and displays of shirts and whistles and a fake float that people can stand on and take a souvenir picture. We pass vendors selling fruit slushes and pretzels and zucchini fries and chocolate peanuts. Buy Now has people dressed as bears juggling in front of their sales booth. As we get closer, I see they juggle Protectors. Hannah freezes as a juggler runs up to us. "Two for one today, girls. What do ya think? Puppies? Kittens?"

"We have ours, thanks," I say as I pull Hannah away. Then I mumble, "Stupid freak," and make us both laugh. Carnival games are everywhere. Hannah spots two booths, Mrs. Malta's Fortune-Telling and Mrs. Malta's Face Paint, and steers me away.

"I know her," she says. "I can't have anyone recognize me."

Our plan is to go to the float-staging area and find Kyle and Leo Cossack. My mom will be there, and I'll convince her to take them to the safety office. Vince Flakeman won't realize they're missing from the float until it's too late. I'll tell her she can get a job doing something else. All that matters is that we're together and safe and away from all this.

Hannah

People fill the streets. Everyone I see is happy and singing to the Broadcaster music. I don't see any protesters, and I wonder if it's all been a strange hoax to test people. Did Melanie's plans fall through when I didn't cooperate? Since Kyle can't lead his group, did they not come?

What I do see are hundreds of Comfort Center officials. They stand four to a block, and each holds the horrible wand. They don't even fake smiles. We find the biggest crowd and walk at a steady pace along with them. We keep our heads down as much as possible as we make our way to where we think the float staging area is located.

Without warning, twenty or thirty people run past us and into the street. In seconds, they form a line shoulder to shoulder, curb to curb, and block parade-goers from crossing. They raise their signs high.

No More Homesteads
No More Protectors
Security, Not Surveillance
Protesting Is a Right

In a flash, Comfort Center officials run toward the protesters from every direction. Jenny pulls on my arm to make me crouch down, but when I spot a long, black braid among the sign-holders, I have to watch. Maria holds a sign that says: *Free*

Leo. Tears blur my vision, and I want to yell, "Run!" but I squeeze Jenny's hand and bite my lip as I watch Maria race across the street. Did she make it? The Broadcaster plays happy-sounding music that muffles the yells of the protesters who are zapped with the chemical that makes them collapse.

"Popcorn! Who needs popcorn?" a vendor asks.

Officials lift the people into a van.

I swallow the scream in my throat.

"Ice-cold lemonade. Lemonade."

In sixty seconds, all the protesters are gone. Forgotten. The streets are again filled with families and children and happy citizens who follow signs and march where they are told to go. I can only hope Maria escaped.

In silence, Jenny and I walk again. After a few more blocks, we see the staging area. We buy drinks from a vendor within viewing distance of the action. We watch the officials at the gate interview people. Everyone needs an ID to get past the barricades and anywhere near the floats.

"I could tell them I'm looking for my mom," Jenny says. "But I don't know if she's back yet."

"What would I do?" I ask.

"You could stay here and—" The words die on Jenny's lips as the Broadcaster blasts out a new report.

Official Report: A girl has been seen aiding the Comfort Center escapee. Anyone knowing her whereabouts must call the nearest Safety Office. Use caution.

A picture of Jenny and me together in our ridiculous hats and sunglasses fills the screen, and then there is a close-up of my face and then her face. Without talking, I grab her hand and move into an alleyway just ahead. "Don't run," I say as we walk down the alley, although my legs are so wobbly I don't think I could anyway.

The alley turns at a street I recognize. I lead Jenny to the park where Jonah took me, and then pull her down to sit close together behind some overgrown bushes. Our bodies shake so badly we hold each other to calm down.

"He found out," Jenny whimpers.

I know she means Vince Flakeman.

"He found out I sent those messages and fired my mom," she says.

"You don't know that."

"My mom wouldn't let anyone put my face on the Broadcaster like that if she could stop it."

"Maybe she's not back yet," I say.

Jenny shakes her head and tears start. "I can't even protect myself," she whispers.

For the first time, I realize that people on the street—any person on the street—may shoot at us. I've only been worried about the Comfort Center personnel catching me. And now I've put Jenny in danger, too.

"You go home," I say. "Find your mom. You can tell everyone I tricked you. I took your Protector and made you come with me. Then you escaped."

Jenny wipes away a tear and looks into my eyes. "Friends don't stop helping each other just because it's hard."

I squeeze her hand and feel my chest relax. "This is more than hard," I say.

"Doesn't matter."

"You might get killed."

"We might get killed."

We lean on each other in silence as our words sink in. Should I go back to Melanie? Do whatever she wants and hope no one gets hurt? Is trying to help Kyle and my dad just a farce?

"Maybe it's all a waste," I say. "It's not really your problem, and what can we do anyway?" I say.

Jenny

I take a deep breath. I think about Governcorp and Protectors and the Homestead and feel my muscles tense. It is *my* problem. "We can't be afraid of Vince Flakeman anymore, and if we stand up to Governcorp, other people will too–that's what the protesters believe, right? That's what Kyle believes and your dad, too."

Hannah nods.

"My mom must not be back from getting that equipment. She'll help us. And you know what else?"

Hannah shakes her head. I think through the words I want to say to make sure I get them right. "If I told that lame story about you stealing my Protector, it would be like saying you're smarter than me."

Hannah stares at me for a second, and then we both roar with laughter. For a few minutes, we're happy like everyone else seems to be. Then another Broadcaster announcement jolts us back.

"We can't get past those parade officials after our pictures showed up so clear on the Broadcaster," Hannah says.

"We need to make ourselves look different, not just stupid hats," I say.

Hannah's face brightens, and she grabs my hand and pulls me up. "Face paint!" she says. "Clowns are always in a parade. Remember the booth? I trust Mrs. Malta. She'll figure out a way to help us."

I nod in agreement, but my knees are wobblier than ever.

Hannah

I declare my trust for Mrs. Malta with more confidence than I feel, and I worry that we're putting her at risk too, but what alternative is there? Jenny and I decide to split up. People will look for two girls together now. I keep the hat over my face as much as possible, even though I know it's giving me a false sense of security. There are many more people in the streets than there were earlier, and walking against the flow makes me more noticeable. I decide to stop at a souvenir booth to wait for a break in the crowd.

"These are darling." The woman next to me picks up a pair of sunglasses with sparkly frames. "Would you mind? They're for my niece."

She holds the glasses out to me, and I realize she wants me to try them on. If I run or say no, I'll just call more attention to myself. I look away and remove my own sunglasses and put the others on as fast as possible.

"Umm," the woman says, studying my face. "I'm not sure." She surprises me and removes the glasses from my face. I gasp and try to hide it with a quick cough. She has a clear view of my face for several seconds before I get my own glasses back in place.

"You look familiar," she says.

My legs want to spring into action. How would a normal person respond?

"Are you Silvia's granddaughter?" she asks.

"No. Sorry," I say. "Excuse me."

I move around her in quick steady steps and reach the street just as passengers emerge from two large buses.

"That was her!" I hear the sunglasses woman holler. "That was her!"

I race behind the bus crowd. There are so many people from the buses that the street is blocked and I'm able to hide in the mix. I move as fast as possible without running until I reach the right intersection. I catch my breath and look across the street to my destination.

Zora's sister is at the face-paint booth, and her brother is selling balloons. Mrs. Malta must be inside the fortune-teller tent. If I walk into the tent and she has a customer, then what? I look for Jenny. We should go in together so I can explain everything. Down the street, a Comfort Center van stops, and the driver talks to two officials on the street. The officials move my way, stopping to talk to people as they walk. Asking questions about me?

I have no choice now. I walk across the street, move the tent flap aside, and enter the booth. The incense and the darkness hit me at the same time. I cough as the smoke fills my nose, and my eyes burn as I try to open them wider to see the room. The purple glow of a glass globe is a few feet away, and the darkness gives it the effect of floating on air. It's the only thing I can see.

"Enter and discover your destiny," a voice says.

I see her robes now and can make out the table under the crystal ball and two chairs.

"Five tokens. Leave your future to me," the voice continues as she waves her hands over the glass globe.

I sit in the chair. "Leave your future to me," the voice says again.

"Mrs. Malta," I whisper. "It's me, Hannah." The hands stop moving, and I see them up close. They are smooth and soft, and the nails are painted with bright, gold polish—Zora.

Before I can even react, a man's voice booms from outside, "We'll check for ourselves." The tent flap lifts.

"Jeez…" The official coughs so hard he steps outside again. "What is that shit?"

Zora grabs me. She shoves me into a corner and pulls a curtain closed in front of me. I push myself against the wall to keep from collapsing. I stop breathing.

I hear the tent flap lift again.

"You got lights in here?" the official says.

"That would take away all the fun," Zora quips. "How about a fortune?"

I see the beam of a flashlight as it shines over the room. I close my eyes and feel my body go stiff.

"Let me see under the table."

I hear Zora pull back the covering.

"What else you got in here?" He kicks something.

I flinch.

"Boxes of cards, candles, wands." I hear Zora open a box. "Lots of incense and maybe some ghosts." She says this in her best mystical voice.

"Weirdo opportunity people." I hear his boots fade and the tent flap rustles.

I'm sweating and light-headed. I hear more voices outside, but I can't understand the words. Suddenly a real light is turned on. The curtain is pulled aside to reveal Zora. And she's pointing a Protector at me.

Jenny

Igive Hannah a head start. I decide to go a few blocks out of the way, and then circle back so I can walk with the crowd in the most congested areas. I try not to listen to the Broadcaster—especially when there's news of a terrorist with red hair. Out of habit, I check for my Protector every time I see one hanging from a stranger's belt. It's a strange emptiness like missing a part of myself. I put my hand in my pocket, pretending it's there. At least I have Shizaru.

A crowd flows from the transit speed station, and I merge into it. I walk next to a family and hope it looks like we belong together. They stop with the rest of the crowd and gaze at the huge Broadcaster near the transit entrance. A band is shown playing a parade march and then as soon as the song is over, the horror appears again.

> **Official Report: A girl has been seen aiding the Comfort Center escapee. Anyone knowing her whereabouts must call the nearest Safety Office. Use your Protectors.**

My heart races in panic as the dad stops to watch. But the little girl on his shoulders says, "Go horsey," and he jogs a few steps and misses my picture.

The little girl claps and laughs.

"Monkeys!" she shouts.

I look where she points. There are just two guys walking. They have on black shirts with a weird white design on the bottom.

"No monkeys," her dad says.

"Lots monkeys," she insists and points again.

The two guys have joined a larger group carrying a sign that reads: Parade Kazoo Band. They all wear the same shirt and big, furry hats that might make them look like monkeys to a little girl. The hats cover most of their faces.

I can play the kazoo.

I slow down. A line of teenagers and young adults stands in front of a table marked *Supplies Here*. A woman gives a snack, shirt, hat, and kazoo to each person. I don't see her asking questions – everyone seems to be in a hurry. I get behind a girl in line, and when it's my turn, I keep my head down and stick out my hand. I put the shirt over my top and as quick as I can, stuff my hair into the hat. I could be anyone.

This disguise is much better than being a clown, and I'll be in the parade for sure. Hannah will figure out that I'm not coming to the face-paint booth. Searching separately might be better anyway. I bite into my energy bar.

"Where's your Protector?" a teenager from the group asks.

"Uh, forgot it?"

"Need one down here, Frizz."

A man walks over and hands me a Protector in a holder. I put it on. I feel my tense shoulders relax. I finally fit in again, and I can protect myself.

Hannah

"What right do you have to put me in danger like this?" Zora demands.

"I don't have any right," I say. I feel the Protector against my ribs. "I thought your mother…"

"You just wanted to put my mother in danger!"

"No. Zora, please. I'll leave."

"Sit down," she demands.

I watch her pace. The Protector is so natural in her hand it looks like an extension of her arm.

I feel hot and cold at the same time, and a sudden dizziness forces me to put my head down. It might be from not eating. It might be from Zora.

"Don't you black-out," she yells. "This little thing scare you?" she laughs as she waves the Protector.

If I lift my head, I'll collapse. I hear Zora reach into a cupboard. She shoves a bottle of juice and a sandwich toward me.

"Thanks," I whisper.

"Don't talk. I'm just figuring out what to do with you."

I take a bite and realize I'm famished. Zora continues pacing, and I try to eat and not think about what could happen. She could turn me in to Governcorp for a reward. How could I blame her when her family is so desperate for money?

"How'd you escape?" she asks.

"Jonah. Do you remember him?"

She half grunts in response. "Where's the other girl? Who is she? Why are you here?"

"The other girl. She might come here too. We split up."

"So, I can get double rewards from Governcorp?"

There's no sarcasm in her voice. All I can think to say is the truth. "You hate them more than anyone."

"Don't tell me what I think or feel. Why are you here?" she asks again.

"My dad is going to be put on a float as an example," I explain. "I need to get him off because—"

"Protesters will make a statement, and most citizens won't like it," Zora finishes.

"He might get killed," I say. "I came here because I need a disguise. I thought…face paint?"

"Wouldn't you look cute?"

"Stop. Will you help or not?"

"You didn't answer my other question. Who's the other girl?"

I realize that Jenny would be here by now if she were coming. Did the Comfort Center officials see her? Do I have to do this by myself?

"Who is she?" Zora commands.

"A born citizen."

"And?"

"She goes to my school."

"And?"

I can't tell Zora that Jenny's mom is the safety officer. I don't want to tell her about Vince Flakeman either.

"Her boyfriend, Kyle – you know Kyle Foster? – will be on a float too. Maybe the same one."

"She's risking her life for some guy?" Zora snorts. Then she imitates the Broadcaster with perfect precision. "*True Love is worth the fight. Smile, and love will blossom.*" Zora laughs. "You know what message I'd give?" In the same eerie Broadcaster voice, she says, "*Suckers deserve what they get,*" and then she storms out.

"Tony," I hear her yell at her brother. "Stand here and don't let anyone in or out."

Now I wish I had refused the sandwich because waiting to know what Zora will do shoots pains to my stomach like a knife. I don't even want to breathe. Where are you, Jenny?

I wait an eternity before the tent flap pulls open, and Zora comes in with a box in her hand.

"Sit over there," she orders.

I move, and Zora opens the box of face paint. I sit still as she covers my face with white makeup. She works next on my lips, eyes, and nose. In no time, she hands me a mirror, and I see my face transformed to a clown with huge lips, black, triangle eyes, a blue nose, red circles for cheeks, and a perpetual smile. She sprinkles glitter all over my hat and gives me a plaid shirt and orange baseball socks that belong to her brother.

Neither of us has said a word.

I want to say something meaningful. I know I can't say thank you. "I saw Maria protesting," I say. Zora fixes her fortune-teller table and doesn't respond. I try again. "I haven't seen any other protesters besides Maria's group. Comfort Center officials came, but I think she escaped." Zora moves boxes, and then she lights some incense. I tell myself I tried, and then I leave.

I walk toward the parade street in a daze. I have no idea what I'll do next. The sound of running makes me turn, hoping to see Jenny.

"Here," Zora says. She hands me a xylophone. It must be one of her brother's toys. "Clowns have to DO something." Before she turns away, she sneers, "Don't get in the way when the protesters show up."

She disappears just as the Broadcaster up ahead shows my picture and then a picture of Jenny and me together. Several people stand and watch. A woman nearby turns and then points to me. I freeze with my mouth half open.

"Look, Maggie," she says to a little girl. "See the cool clown?"

Jenny

As part of the kazoo band, I march into the parade-staging area. Everyone seems to understand some plan except for me. I hear pieces of conversation: front of grandstand, backups, monkeys. Monkeys?

I pretend to clean out my kazoo and move closer to a conversation.

"It's his plan; where the hell is Jonah?"

"And what's that shit on the Broadcaster? 'Kyle Foster is not a criminal.' Who authorized that?"

"Yeah. If that crap keeps playing, no one will be taken off guard. They'll start using Protectors right away."

I never thought my messages could be dangerous or harmful. They're supposed to make people think and ask questions. I need to find Kyle right now.

"Where you going?" yells Frizz, the man in charge who gave me the Protector.

"Restroom!" I yell back as I begin my search.

I pass a pirate ship float, a gingerbread house, and a replica of the Garden of Eden with the biggest plastic snake I've ever seen. Band members with flutes and drums and trombones gather in groups, and then more floats–Homestead House Builders, Homestead Teachers, Citizens for Technology. There are so many floats. Which one could hold Kyle and Leo Cossack? I'll never find them in this mess.

I walk a little farther and see a boy in the Safety Academy blazer. I follow him and watch as he climbs onto the float where I'd imagined myself. My stomach sinks. All the cadets look like perfect professionals as they stand tall and listen to an Academy official. She tells them how much they've achieved and how honored they should be. She tells them how following laws is so important and how much she loves her job and they will too. Then she answers a few questions about the parade and the party afterward. I look at my stupid, black shirt and try to remember what matters.

"Kazoo-player!" a female official with long, silver hair yells at me. "You are way out of position. Staging is back this way." She checks her respond-pad and motions for me to follow.

"Do you have a printout of the parade order?" I ask.

The Broadcaster music plays right in the middle of my question.

"What?" the woman asks.

I try again as we walk.

"We need a printout of the float order."

"No, you don't." She stops and looks at me. "And who's 'we'?" She narrows her eyes at me. I want to say never mind, but this could be my last chance to find Kyle before it's too late.

"I want to meet one of my friends after the parade," I try. "She's on the Opportunity Float."

"Meet a friend?" The woman looks puzzled. I hear voices a few feet away and turn to see Jade's dad stepping up onto the Governcorp float. He sits down next to Vince Flakeman. I want to forget my question and escape, but the woman pulls my arm and turns me toward her and away from the Governcorp people. "What is this?" she says. "Did Frizz send you?" I try to steady my breath. Who is this woman? Why is it such a big deal to ask about the floats?

"We can't have confusion over there," she says in a strange, quiet voice.

I mimic her quiet tone. "We're just making sure," I say.

"Celebration of Fun, Governcorp, Opportunity, and then Kazoo band."

"Melanie!" a voice hollers. It's Vince Flakeman.

She steps toward him, and I turn away. I keep my eyes on an eight-foot cardboard version of the Queen of Hearts that is part of a float straight ahead. Not too fast. Not too slow. Six steps maybe? Step. Step.

"How long do I stay on this piece of junk?" Flakeman asks.

Step. Step.

"I arranged something for you," the woman says. "At the grandstand, you will get out and say a few words in front of the Opportunity float."

Step. Step. I duck behind the Queen. I breathe a sigh of relief. I'm hidden, but I can still hear.

"Good. That sounds perfect," Flakeman says.

I put Flakeman out of my mind a second and concentrate on the good news. The Opportunity float will be close to the kazoos. There's a good chance Kyle will be on that one. I peek at Flakeman and see he's turned away from me. I step out of my hiding place, look a few feet ahead, and gasp. Susan's heading right for me! I move back into the shadows of the Queen cut-out, and I pull the hat over my face as far as I can without suffocating. I see her coming closer, and I pretend to tie my shoe.

My announcements blast the air from a nearby Broadcaster, and I close my eyes as Susan stops right in front of me.

Official report: Hannah Cossack is not a terrorist. Leave your Protectors at home. Kyle Foster is not a criminal.

I tie my other shoe. Will it ever end? Won't Susan go away?

Official report: Protectors kill.

Flakeman is swearing so loud I hear him through the announcement.

Official report: Leo Cossack is not a criminal.

Susan laughs. I tell myself not to look up even though I'm dying to. I can feel the grin spread over my face and I bite my lip, so I don't laugh along with her. Flakeman continues his rave. Maybe I should I reveal myself and ask for help? Before I can decide, Susan marches toward Flakeman as he yells again.

"What do you mean Morgan's not back yet? Get that blasphemy off the Broadcaster!"

My heart jumps. My mom doesn't know what's going on. I know she'll figure out a way to get my face off the Broadcaster and help Hannah. As I sneak away, I can hear the laughter in Susan's voice as she asks Flakeman, "What's the matter? A little Broadcaster mal-function?"

Hannah

I discover little kids either cry when they see me or want to touch my face. I decide to be the kind of clown who doesn't talk; I just play songs on my xylophone. Red, red, blue. Red, red, blue. Yellow, yellow, yellow, yellow, purple, orange, green. Repeat endlessly.

The crowds yell at the Broadcaster whenever the parade music is interrupted. They have the same reaction whether it's Jenny's announcements or the announcements about two girl escapees. They don't care about either. I even hear a woman yell out, "Shut the Broadcaster up! Let us party and have fun!" What will they do if protesters stop the parade? My mind wonders to Jonah. Where is he?

A boy shakes my shirt and interrupts my thoughts. I mime, *hello*.

"Play the Safety song," he pleads. I begin to wave good-bye when a Comfort Center official walks up.

"Yeah, play the Safety song," the official says. "Everyone knows that."

I rack my brain thinking of the tune my sisters sang. Even if I remember it, I won't know the notes. Think.

The boy smiles in anticipation. I'm thankful the painted smile on my face masks the panic inside. I hear Jonah's voice in my head. You're a natural. You're a natural. I hand my hammer to the little boy and he pounds out some notes and sings. The official grunts and walks away. After a few minutes, I take back the hammer and wave goodbye. I move to a denser part of the crowd, and exhale again.

Moving gives me confidence. A clown is a natural participant in the parade. I've proven that. I'll walk right into the street and play my non-song until I find my dad. Even if I just yell, "I love you!" to him, it will be worth it.

Jenny

I race back to the kazoo band with the grin still on my face. It was nice to see Flakeman laughed at, and even better, Kyle and Mr. Cossack will be near the Kazoo band if they're on the Opportunity float.

Frizz sees I've come back and points to a place in line. We practice turns and marching straight, but I'm continually out of step.

"Pay attention," a girl says as I bump into her for the third time instead of turning like I'm supposed to.

My mind is too full. Now I wish Hannah and I had stayed together. It will take both of us to figure out how to get Kyle and Leo–and us–to safety. How will we get them off the float? When will my mom get back?

"What group are you?" the same girl asks as we stop for a break.

Group? It could be a letter or animal or color or person's name. Maybe a number? I give the easiest answer. "Group one."

"For real? Wow."

Group one is something important?

"What group are you?" I ask.

"Ten," she says.

I must have a funny look on my face because she touches my arm and says, "Don't worry. We won't run. And there's a rumor that some people will have real Protectors if we need them."

I nod and try to swallow, but the knot in my throat won't let me.

Why have I been so stupid? I look again at my Protector. No wonder it's so light. It's a fake. I'm with the protesters!

The girl's face goes out of focus, and I wobble against another kazoo player.

"You okay?" someone asks.

"Let her sit down."

I get to the ground just in time and put my head between my knees.

"Should I get Frizz?"

I shake my head.

Someone hands me a water bottle, and I take a gulp. I inhale. I exhale. I focus on my feet but slowly raise my eyes. I blink a few times–do I really see monkeys on everyone's shirt? I look down at my own. How did I not see them before? I feel my insides quiver and I fight the urge to rip off the shirt and hat and just hide behind a dumpster somewhere and wait until my mom finds me.

"Better?" the girl asks.

The figurine in my pocket pokes my butt. Kyle is still in trouble and hasn't done anything wrong.

I take another drink. "I'm good," I say as I stand. "When will the people with real Protectors show up?"

"Maybe in front of the grandstand?" She shrugs. "Just a rumor."

I nod.

The girl shivers and rubs her arms. "I hope it doesn't hurt too much," she says in a quiet voice. "The Comfort Center wands."

I nod again and feel my knees shake as the Broadcaster blasts music over our heads and stops any chance of more conversation.

Hannah

I reach the hill overlooking the parade street and watch the first float go by. I walk down the steep incline and pass families on blankets enjoying their picnic. I wave to the kids who point at me. As I get nearer to the bottom, I tell people I'm part of the show and inch my way through the crowd to get close to the curb. I stop just short of the street. If I step off the curb, I step into a spotlight I don't want. I never wanted. And once I'm in the light, I can't go back.

I watch a float approach. It's called Home Sweet Home. It's a replica of the outside of a Homestead apartment building. Flowerpots line the perimeter and a happy family of four waves to the crowd. I recognize them. The Marquis. Their little girl, Terese, played with my sisters in the Homestead. I'm sure they need the money Governcorp pays them to smile for the crowd.

I set my jaw, stand straight, and march into the street.

Comfort Center officials glance my way, but I wave at the crowd like a professional.

I walk among the floats and look for Kyle and my dad. Retirement Heaven, One Minute Fitness, Homestead Teachers, rock bands, banjo music, dance ensemble, Buy Now. I scan the crowded curbs and hillside for Jenny every chance I get.

Thirty minutes of waving to the crowd is exhausting. Where are you, Jenny? Kyle? Dad? We need to be together. The heat is causing my makeup to drip, and without a mirror, I'm afraid to blot it. Popcorn and hot-dog vendors make me hungry again, my feet hurt, and I'd give anything for a glass of water.

Official report: Hannah Cossack is not a terrorist. Leave your Protectors at home. Kyle Foster is not a criminal.

"Keep the music on!"

"Shut the thing up!"

The announcements continue and so do the angry yells from the crowd.

"Turn it off!"

"Stop the noise!"

"Catch the damn terrorists!"

I hold my breath each time the announcement plays. This time when my picture comes on the screen, a blast rings out, and I kneel in terror, sure I'll be killed in the next second. The crowd cheers and I realize the shot was aimed at the Broadcaster. The screen is black. A Comfort Center official grabs the man who fired the shot. The crowd boos and defends him until the official zaps a few people with his wand. Then everyone turns away.

"Watch out, clown!"

I turn and see the next float bearing down on me. I've been standing in the street without moving. I jump onto the curb. I take a deep breath and make myself wave to the kids nearby. I have to get a drink. How? Where? I look up the hill and see restroom signs. Will I miss too much of the parade to search for a fountain? The float that almost hit me grinds to a stop. The Comfort Center officials have stopped the procession to clear away the troublemakers.

I climb towards the restroom signs as fast as I can, but when I reach the top all I find are people in line for portable toilets and no drinkable water. I wet my parched lips with my tongue and glance at a half empty soda bottle in the trash. I groan at the idea, but I start for the bin. The sight of the back of a tall boy just a few feet away stops me in my tracks. Russell! A tear starts down my cheek, and I restrain myself from running, but when I reach him, I can't help but touch his arm as I whisper, "It's me, Russell. Hannah."

He opens his eyes wide. "Wow."

"You in line?" a guy behind us yells.

We move out of the way and stare at each other.

"Your hair is showing on the side," Russell says. "And the white stuff is dripping off your face. You must be hot."

I nod. It's all I can do to hold off a sob.

He hands me his drink, and I gulp so fast I can feel the liquid hit my stomach. We walk away from several viewers and finally sit under a tree with low branches. It's the best we can do for camouflage.

"I was so thirsty," I say. "Thanks."

Russell plays with his shoelaces and says, "The sense of thirst means that dehydration has already started." He looks up at me. "I can get you more."

"I'm fine now." The Broadcaster flashes another picture of Jenny and me, and I close my eyes.

"You shouldn't be here," Russell says.

I realize how selfish I've been to put him in danger. "I'm sorry. I was just so glad to see you. I shouldn't have—"

"I don't mean that. I just mean…officials are everywhere."

"My dad and Kyle are on a float," I say. "We need to get them off."

"You and Jenny?"

"Yeah."

"Is she a clown, too?"

"I don't know. We got separated."

"What float are they on? Your dad and Kyle."

"I don't know that either," I say. I let my head slump against the tree and wish I could disappear in the branches.

"You should drink some more," Russell says with a wrinkled brow. I do as he says, but the drink doesn't improve my spirit. Our plan is not even a plan.

Russell pulls out his respond-pad and pulls up the parade information. He flips through a list of float titles and descriptions.

"Based on the information listed, I'd say your dad and Kyle will be on one of these floats: Governcorp, Opportunity, or Courthouse Replica."

Russell's voice is steady and sure, and he looks at me with a shy but confident smile. I nod and feel a surge of hope again. I finish the drink and sit up just as the crowd near the street lets out a cheer. The parade is on the move again.

"Are those floats in front of us or behind?" I ask.

"They're in the middle of the parade. If you go by the grandstand, they should be there in five minutes or so."

I can make out the tall bleachers of the grandstand from where we are. "Thanks for your help, Russell."

He points to my hair, and I stuff it back into my hat as best I can. He nods. I smile and nod back.

"I'll watch for Jenny," he says looking at his shoe.

I give him a peck on the cheek, squeeze his hand, and then head down the block.

Jenny

Like everyone else in the kazoo band, I watch floats go by as we wait for our turn to enter the parade. The floats' motors have sensors to break or speed-up automatically, so they keep an even distance apart. The Celebration of Fun float turns a corner and rolls in front of me. It's elaborate, just like Jade promised. The Ferris wheel is huge, and the merry-go-round has exotic animals to sit on. It takes several minutes for me to spot Jade. It seems so weird that she doesn't stand out at all. Each person waves when they get to the top of the Ferris wheel, just like the person before them. Round and round and round. Nothing changes.

Governcorp officials are on the next float. A huge sign that reads Success for All hangs from the float, and the officials smile and throw Buy Now coupons to the crowd. Vince Flakeman is the cheeriest of them all.

And then the Opportunity Float. It's bigger and better than I thought it would be–twice as big as the other floats. Everyone is holding an I'm a New Citizen or I'm a Buddy sign. I see lots of kids I know, and I almost jump and wave before I catch myself. The float has tiers of steps. Each step shows part of the citizenship process. On the very top is a huge citizen certificate and cardboard Protector. There's no way to tell if Kyle is on board without getting closer.

Our kazoo leader marches us forward, and I hum into my instrument, faking my way through the song. The Broadcaster music is interrupted again by my messages, and someone in the crowd yells, "Get the terrorists!" People cheer. No one is listening to what I wrote.

I scan the crowd. Where are you, Hannah?

In between songs, kazoo members whisper as if they're playing a giant game of telephone. When the message reaches my row, I hear "Group One hops on after the turn at Olive. Keep playing and make it part of the show."

Hops on what?

The girl next to me says, "I'm glad it had lots of steps."

I'm supposed to hop on the Opportunity float on purpose? This is too good to be true.

Hannah

I walk back into the street towards the grandstand. The Celebration of Fun float moves by me. The Ferris wheel has stalled. I stifle a laugh when I spot Jade and her clones sweating in their seats. The Broadcaster plays Jenny's message.

"Shut the Broadcaster up for the parade!" a man hollers and runs right in front of me to hurl a rock at the Broadcaster. A Comfort Center official charges out of the crowd and knocks the man cold with his stunning wand.

"Move!" the official hollers at me, and he and his partner pick up the man and drag him away. I run toward the next float heading for the grandstand. It's the Governcorp float. My hands shake as I play on the xylophone. I can't even play my non-tune; I just go up and down the scale and glance over to see who's on the float. I see Vince Flakeman smile and wave to the crowd, and even though I'm desperate to find my dad, I'm glad that I don't see him with this group.

The Governcorp float stops at the grandstand, and Flakeman gets off. The parade procession comes to a halt again. I keep walking and see the Opportunity float—another place Russell said to check. The kids on the float have set down their signs and are talking or fooling around as they wait for the parade to start up again. The float would be easy to climb on. Should I? It might be my only chance.

My heart speeds up as I step on board. I move deliberately around the perimeter as I scan the float. I square my shoulders. A few kids give me a second look but ask no questions. I see a set of steps that lead to the second level and move faster as I notice the shiny new Protectors around everyone's waist.

The height allows a breeze to reach me and a few clouds give some relief from the sun. I can see the whole parade stretched out in front and behind the Opportunity float and hear all the echoes from the Broadcasters. The grandstand is packed. I walk to the end of the float, but there's no sign of Kyle or my dad.

"What're you doin'?" a gruff voice asks from behind.

An image of a Protector pointed at my head rushes through my brain, but I keep my voice steady as I turn around to show my smiling clown face. A guy not much older than I am in a Governcorp uniform looks me up and down. At least his Protector is in a holder. He blocks my way to the steps.

"Nothing," I say as I shrug. "I thought my friend…Jade would be here."

He folds his arms and cocks his head.

"That so?"

I take a step to leave, and he moves to block my path. He wants me to glance at his Protector sticking out, but I refuse to look at anything but his beady, bug eyes.

"You look really stupid." He grabs my hat and throws it down to the next level. My ponytail flops down just like my picture on the Broadcaster.

"Play the Safety song, *clown*," he sneers.

"That song is in a minor key," I say with as much authority as I can. "This wouldn't play the notes." I push my way past him, but he grabs the xylophone and slams it down.

"What good is it then?" He laughs and snorts and then walks away. "Pick that mess up and get off before I call the Comfort Center."

My heart sinks as I look at the broken instrument. I bend down and touch it, and even though it seems silly, I don't know if I can keep going without it. Where will my courage come from? I stand and take a deep breath. Storm clouds are visible in the distance, and a cool breeze hits my face. Rain might stop the parade, and then I'll never find my dad. My arms drop to my side. I'm tired and…empty. The wind surges, and with it comes a strange humming sound. It sounds like a swarm of bees. I look down the street. A kazoo band? I make myself blink because I can't believe my eyes. Rows of people in monkey shirts. Sixty? Eighty? I count across – two, four, six, eight, twelve? I count the total rows – five, ten, fifteen, at least twenty! Hundreds of protesters in plain sight ready to march toward the grandstand. The protesters are here! I run down the rest of the stairs hoping against all hope. Could Jonah possibly be with them? Can he help me find my dad?

Jenny

We begin the march again and play our kazoos.

"Group One, Go!" Frizz yells, and I jog with the other kazoo players toward the Opportunity float. The plan I've heard is to hop on and get the crowd and kids on the float to sing along. As we jog, a familiar voice echoes from somewhere nearby.

"*This is Kyle Foster. I was not a good citizen. Don't commit crimes. Follow the rules.*" I slow down. Where is that coming from? Not the Broadcasters—it's not loud enough.

"*Protesters without permits must go home. Enjoy the parade. There's nothing to protest.*"

Several other kazoo players slow down too and shout in confusion.

"What's that?"

"Are we still climbing on?"

"I don't get it."

"Keep going," an older girl shouts as she pushes a few people toward the Opportunity float.

Did the voice come from the float behind me? Kyle's voice? I feel a surge of adrenaline as I concentrate on listening again.

"*This is Leo Cossack. I failed my citizenship duties. Always use your Protector to stop criminals. Protectors save lives. Viewers keep us safe.*"

The sound *is* from behind me. The float must have its own speakers. I found them! I skip to the curb to wait for the rest of the kazoos to go by. I can hop on the float, and then…then…I'll figure it out.

"Down in front," someone yells, and I scrunch down as much as possible even though my body wants to jump up and shout. The kazoo band takes forever to march by. Finally, the last row passes and only a half block away is the float approaching with Kyle and Mr. Cossack. I stand up on my tiptoes to see.

"This is my spot!" a woman yells.

"Sorry, I'll leave in just a—"

She shoves me into the street, and I fall. I get up ready to yell at the woman until I think twice. I rub my elbow and knee. I feel beads of sweat on my forehead. I'm smack in-between the kazoos and the Courthouse float, alone in the street where everyone can see me.

Which way do I run?

The Broadcaster plays music again as I see someone jump down from the Opportunity float and run in my direction. Her ponytail is loose, and I see white face paint on her cheeks.

"Hannah!" I scream and then fling my hands over my mouth as I realize what I've done. I can only hope the Broadcaster music has drowned out my yell. I'm too far away for Hannah to have seen or heard me anyway. Groups of people in the crowd scream. Are they yelling for someone to catch her? I see officials waving wands at three men with "Close the Homestead" signs. The men run and the crowd cheers on the officials as they race to zap the men.

Now's my chance.

I run the half block towards the kazoo band and hope Hannah is running there too. I weave through the rows of kazoo players and say 'sorry, sorry,' more times than I can count. When I reach the front, I see Hannah a few feet away in the street, and I wave both my arms frantically.

"Here," I yell. "Over here."

She's out of breath as we grab on to each other and move back into the rows of kazoo players.

"You made—"

Frizz grabs my arm and turns me around before I finish. "What's going on?" he demands.

How do I answer? My brain goes blank as I stare at his angry eyes.

"Remember me?" Hannah asks. "A friend of Jonah's? Is he here?"

Frizz frowns as he studies Hannah, but before he can respond, Kyle's voice echoes through the speakers again.

"This is Kyle Foster. I was not a good citizen. Don't commit crimes. Follow the rules. Protesters without permits must go home. Enjoy the parade. There's nothing to protest."

"What's wrong with that kid?" Frizz mumbles.

"Governcorp is making him," I say. "He might be chained to the float."

"How would *you* know?" Frizz spats.

"This is Leo Cossack. I failed my citizenship duties. Always use your Protector to stop criminals. Protectors save lives. Viewers keep us safe."

Hannah gasps at the sound of her father's voice and turns toward the float. "They're on the float behind us?" I nod, and Hannah turns to Frizz. "Can you help get them off?" she asks.

"Opportunity Float is at the grandstand!" a band member yells.

Frizz drops my arm and runs to assemble groups. We're on our own. Hannah and I walk to the last row of the kazoo players to get a full view of the float behind us.

The float is a replica of an old stone-and-brick Courthouse built in Middletown in the 1900s. The sign on the building reads, *The Rule of Law Keeps Everyone Safe*. In front of the building sits a giant judge's bench, and on either side of it is a long, straight sitting area. There are two people, one on each side of the float.

"It must be them," I say. "Come on!"

"It's too high," Hannah argues.

"We'll climb up." I take a step, but Hannah pulls me back into the kazoos.

"Are you afraid?" I ask. "I'm not."

"Jenny!" she says, holding my shirt. "The float is at least five feet off the ground, and there are no visible steps. We'll be standing in the middle of the street."

My brain knows she's right, and I feel bad to have accused her of being scared. We're both scared. "We can't just leave them out there," I say.

"Get in position to march!" a kazoo leader yells.

Kyle's voice booms in our ears again from the float.

"What did they do to make him say those things?" Hannah asks.

"It's a recording," I remind her. "People see him, so they believe he's saying it."

"If the parade stops again…and the float is closer…?" she asks.

I nod. "You can boost me," I say.

"We can march with the protesters until the right chance comes," Hannah says. 'March with the protesters'–even though I've been doing it, the thought still gives me a chill.

"You know how to get them unlocked, right?"

I swallow hard. Why haven't I thought about that? If a fingerprint was used to verify the lock, I'd never get it off. If Flakeman locked them? If my mom locked them? The only codes I know are the ones Carmichael uses. I just have to hope.

"Yeah. Of course," I say.

Hannah

Jenny and I walk next to a girl too scared to ask us questions. The protesters play the Safety song, and the crowd sings along as we march closer and closer to the grandstand.

Official Report: Anyone knowing the whereabouts of this girl must call the nearest saf—

A Broadcaster nearby shuts off, but the rest of the announcement echoes from the Broadcasters ahead of us.

Official report: Leo Cossa—

Another Broadcaster goes dead? That can't be a coincidence. I look across the street and see wires from a Broadcaster hanging limp. "Look," I say as I point it out to Jenny.

"My mom!" Jenny jumps and points. "There she is walking to the next one."

We see her mom dismantle another and then she ducks out of view.

Jenny's eyes light up. "The Broadcaster won't be able to tell people to look for us," she says.

I nod, but when there're so many machines, what good will dismantling just a few do?

The Opportunity float has stopped in front of the grandstand, and our kazoo group marches to within feet of it. Without a word, our neat marching rows dissolve as kazoo players edge closer to each other and toward the float.

Vince Flakeman stands on the grandstand and speaks into a microphone. His voice booms through the nearby, undamaged Broadcaster.

"Welcome, Middletown citizens, to this outstanding anniversary parade."

Cheers erupt, and he smiles and waves. "The Comfort Center officials did find a few rogue protesters among us," he says.

The crowd hisses and boos.

"But they have been taken care of and will be treated at the Center."

Cheers again.

"We celebrate our Homesteads," Flakeman continues. "They offer opportunity people jobs, education, medical care, and a quick path to citizenship in our glorious city and country. Everyone who works hard can become a citizen."

The Courthouse float is very close behind us. Everyone can hear Kyle's recorded voice.

"This is Kyle Foster. I was not a good citizen. Don't commit crimes. Follow the rules. Protesters without permits must go home. Enjoy the parade. There's nothing to protest."

"Unlike that young man," Flakeman says, "I invite our new citizens and buddies to come and receive a ribbon of success."

The Courthouse float is so close now, I see Kyle limp across and then fall; a chain is on his leg. I gasp, and this time it's Jenny who grabs me so I don't run out.

"Let's go now," I plead.

"It's still moving," Jenny says. "A few more seconds."

I see a person hunched over on a bench. I wipe away a tear. My poor father.

"Maybe there are steps on the sides?" Jenny says.

"I'll go to my dad's side. You go by Kyle?"

Jenny nods. We wait and watch the kids on the Opportunity float get off and stand in line for an official to put a medal around their necks.

Flakeman yells into the microphone, "Young people like you will not let your fellow citizens down."

The distribution of medals ends, and kids stand in a line and wait for Flakeman to finish his speech.

"Wear this proudly to—"

Flakeman's voice cuts off. The Opportunity float moves away from the grandstand platform and glides across the street to the opposite curb. It seems like a strange fluke or mechanical failure until several kazoo players go into the street and lie down. It's part of a plan! A voice booms from a loudspeaker at the top of the Opportunity float.

"Opportunity people demand the Homestead be closed!" The voice is clear and strong, and even though I don't see him, my heart jumps because I know it's Jonah. He made it out of the Comfort Center. He made it!

It takes the Comfort Center officers a moment to comprehend the situation, and in their delay, the rest of the kazoo protesters run to their places in the street. They all lie down and form a human barrier around the float. Officials use their wands, and protesters scream as they're hit. The grandstand crowd stands to watch. Some cheer the Comfort Center people on. A few try to either interfere or help the officials–it's hard to tell which–but in all cases, they get hit themselves with the body-stunning fluid.

"Now!" Jenny yells, and we race to the Courthouse float.

My dad sits on the bench bent over like a broken manikin. He's tethered just like Kyle. Tears flow down my cheeks, and with them, a feeling of helplessness; to see my proud father's head drop to his chest, his shoulders slumped, his voice not even his. I take a deep breath, and wipe the tears away with my sleeve. I can't feel sorry for my dad or have him feel sorry for himself or me when we need to fight.

"Dad!" I yell. "I'm getting you off."

He looks my way with his mouth open and then stands, reaches his arms out and comes as close as the chain allows. His eyes come back to life, and I feel all the strength I need in one word.

"Hannah."

Jenny

The fake Kyle message screams from the speaker again.

"I didn't say those things!" Kyle yells. "Protesting is a right."

I can hear his real voice, but no one else is close enough.

"Kyle!" I yell. "Can you hear me?"

I can see over the top of the float but not if I get too close. He limps closer to the edge and then jumps back when he sees me. I hope it's because I've surprised him and not because he's afraid of me. But how could I blame him?

"Are you all right?" I ask.

"I can say what I want," he insists. "Haven't you done enough?"

"I'm sorry. I'm sorry I didn't stick up for you in the safety office," I say.

Kyle turns away.

"I'm sorry," I say again. He still won't respond. "Hannah's here!" I yell.

"What do you mean, here?" he says, looking down at me.

"We're getting you off."

The voice booms from the other float again. "Opportunity people want fair wages and decent housing. We want Protectors banned, and officials held accountable. Guns kill."

I look back and see Comfort Center officials attempt to climb onto the Opportunity float. They zap people lying on the ground who block their path, but that only makes it worse. There is no space to move the stunned bodies. The ocean of shirts is everywhere. Screams of pain ring out among the protesters as the fluid hits them or the Comfort Center people step on them. But they stay put.

People in the crowd yell. "We want the parade!" "Get rid of the protesters!"

"Peaceful protesting is part of democracy," the voice from the float says.

Sirens screech as more Comfort Center officials arrive in vans. They pull stunned protesters away.

"Hurry up, or we'll take care of them!" I hear someone scream from the crowd.

"You can't even find two girls," shouts someone else.

I have to hurry before people notice Hannah and I are in the street. Before Flakeman notices we are trying to free his prisoners. I throw my hat off and reach my arms to the top of the float and hang on, but I'm not strong enough to pull myself up.

"Hannah!" I shout as I let go.

She runs from the other side of the float. "There are no stairs anywhere," she says.

"Is there a code pad to release your chain?" I yell to Kyle.

"Yes," he says. "But I can't reach it."

"Can you reach my hand?"

He tries, and our fingertips touch, but that does no good. He can't pull me up.

Hannah holds her hands like a stirrup and tries to boost me up, but I can't get on board the float. I try the same with her, but the float is too high and the surface slippery.

"Protesters without permits are committing an illegal activity," Vince Flakeman shouts into his microphone. "These protesters are interrupting a community event where you," he turns and waves to the Grandstand crowd, "have a right to have fun and enjoy watching your child go by on a float or in a band."

The parade crowd cheers.

"We vote in our country, and in the future, if you, our loyal citizens, want to change Homestead or Protector laws, who am I to stop you?" Flakeman continues. "You and only you can protect your citizenship rights in the polls and on the streets."

"Keep the Homesteads!" a man in the grandstand yells.

"Protectors keep us strong!" shouts someone else.

"Protectors are our right!"

"Homesteads mean jobs!"

I can't take my eyes of Flakeman as he waves his arms and nods his head every time a citizen shouts.

Hannah shakes me. "We have to try again. Hurry."

I put my foot in her cupped hand and jump up as she boosts me. I hold on and swing my right leg. The middle of my foot snags the platform edge, and I strain, arms shaking, to pull my torso even with the float.

Flakeman keeps on, "Why should good citizens like you sit here and—"

BOOM!

The explosion sends me tumbling to the ground as a huge electric bolt shoots up like a firecracker across the street. Was there a lightning strike from the clouds that have moved in? I look over and see two people. My mom and Susan stand by the large, steel box where the explosion came from. Hannah helps me up, and we watch as my mom forces open a door in the box and pulls out wires with some tool.

BOOM!

More bolts of fire fly from the booth, and my mom is thrown to the ground. "Mom!" I yell through another explosion. I start to run toward her, but Hannah pulls me back.

"Wait," Hannah orders.

We watch Susan pull my mom up by the hand. She's okay.

Everyone in the crowd looks stunned and stands in place, silent. The silence is eerie. No one seems to know what to do next. I see Vince Flakeman shake his microphone and talk into it. No sound comes out. My mom holds a big cone-like thing to her mouth.

"The parade is over," she says. Her voice is strong and almost as loud as the sound from the other speakers. The crowd mumbles. "Slowly clear the grandstand," she says with authority.

"Parade protesters, slowly walk home. The courts are the place for this. The courts. Not the streets."

People murmur to each other, and a few get up and start down the grandstand steps. Most people stay put with arms folded and stare at the Comfort Center people loading vans with immobilized protesters.

"Clear the grandstand," my mom says again. "Go home peacefully," she hollers through the cone. A few more people walk down the steps. I feel the tension in my muscles loosen.

"It will be okay," I say to Hannah as I grab her arm. We watch another group of people head down the grandstand steps. I turn to see how Kyle is doing.

"Flakeman!" Hannah gasps.

I raise my head and see him throw down the microphone and scramble toward my mom with a Protector raised in the air. "Mom!" I yell. I wave my arms and jump up and down, and I think she sees me, but then I realize so does everyone else.

"Those girls!" someone yells.

We scrunch down, but before anyone can use a Protector against us, a door under the Opportunity float bursts open. Three men and the woman with silver hair appear like Trojan soldiers. Flakeman stands right in front of their pointed Protectors. Behind them is an army of people that were hiding in the float. The rapid blasts of shots come again and again, and Flakeman hits the ground.

Everyone screams. Everyone runs. Everyone shoots.

Shots fly around us. It's chaos and noise and confusion and blood and screams. Hannah and I duck in the deepest corner under the float. We see a pair of man's legs run toward us, and we clutch each other. My heart is beating louder than the echo of shots and screams. The legs stop, and the person swings up onto the float.

"No," I scream. I run from my hiding spot. "Don't shoot!" I look up fearing a Protector in my face, but instead, I see Russell pull and tug on Kyle's chains.

"Russell!" I yell, relief flooding me. "Find the code pad. Try 123456."

"Not a secure password," he says.

"Russell!" Hannah and I yell together.

He shakes his head. "Wrong."

I can't think. I can't think. "Try ABCXYZ."

"That's a little better," Russell says. "Didn't work though."

Hannah looks at me with a pained stare.

"I'm trying!" I say.

"I know," Hannah says. "Just hurry."

Protectors go off all around us, and the screaming isn't from fear anymore; now it's from people in pain. Grandstand people run into the street or try to climb the hill, but there are so many people panicking, they begin to run over each other. I'm going to get killed. We're going to get killed. Where's my mom?

"Any other ideas?" Russell shouts down.

Hannah grabs me and turns me around, so I will look at her and not the chaos. "Jenny," she says in a firm but not too loud voice. "Concentrate on me. Just me."

Her face is still a mess with all the paint, but I can see her clear, truthful eyes and she grabs my hands, and I nod.

"Just think," she says looking straight at me.

Sirens screech as more Comfort Center officials arrive. I can't think. Is my mom okay? Susan was helping her. Are they friends again?

Hannah squeezes my hands. "What is another code Carmichael uses?"

I shake my head. "I can't remember."

"Close your eyes," Hannah says softly. "Just breathe."

I do what she says, and my mom's face pops into my head then Susan's face and I remember her laugh when I was hiding behind the cardboard queen. The Queen of Hearts.

"Cards," I yell as my eyes fly open. "Try *cards*, Russell."

"Not enough characters."

I count letters on my fingers.

"*Tricks*. Try *tricks*!" I shout.

A moment later Kyle yells, "It worked!"

"There's another protester!" A man points at us as he and his friend run toward me. I look down. I'm still in the monkey shirt.

"Hurry!" Hannah yells to Russell.

Kyle sits on the edge of the float, and Hannah and I help him down, so he won't hurt his bandaged leg. Russell unlocks Leo Cossack's tether with the same code, and Mr. Cossack jumps down.

"It's those girls," shouts one of the men. He stands just feet away, waving his Protector at us.

"We don't have Protectors. Leave us alone!" I shout.

The man laughs. "You just admitted breaking another law."

That's just what I would have said a few days ago. The thought makes me shiver. The man raises his Protector, and as I scream, Russell jumps down in front of me.

BANG. BANG.

Everything moves in slow motion. Russell falls to the ground near my feet, and I see one of the men point his Protector again.

BANG. BANG.

Am I hit? I look up and see my mom lower her Protector. The two men fall to my right.

"Russell!" Hannah shouts as she bends down to his side. Blood oozes from his chest, and his face is blank, and the red…red…red.

I take off my monkey shirt and press it against his chest where the blood oozes. "You'll be okay, Russell," I say, looking into his eyes.

My mom grabs his arms, and Mr. Cossack grabs his legs. They carry him out of the street and away from the worse part of the chaos. Mr. Cossack offers my mom his shirt, and she expertly presses it against the wound in Russell's chest. "Breathe slowly, Russell," my mom says as she moves a piece of hair from his eyes.

Hannah and I kneel on either side of him, and we each grab one of his hands. I choke on my words. "You saved us, Russell."

His lip quivers up on one side, and he shakes his head a little in denial.

"You did, Russell. I'm sorry I didn't think of the password faster. You can always help me think of passwords from now on, okay?"

He nods his head slightly, and then his eyes roll back. "Russell?" I say. "Russell! Make him be okay!" I yell to my mom. "He has to be okay."

She breathes over and over into his mouth. The shirts on his chest are soaked through. "Come on, Russell," she pleads. "Come on, breathe!" Sweat forms on her brow as she tries again and again. She wipes a tear from her cheek, looks at me, and shakes her head. She closes Russell's eyes.

I sob with so much pain that my head pounds and my lungs hurt. I know there's noise and chaos everywhere, but all I hear is Russell's funny sayings and see his smile, and I grab onto him again. "Please, Russell. *Please.*"

My mom hugs me and then tries to pull me away, but I won't move.

Hannah

I sob on Russell's shoulder. Of all the people to get hurt, why did it have to be Russell? Did he understand how much he meant to me? I think of the day he stood up for me against Flakeman. "You're the bravest person I know, Russell," I whisper into his ear. "I'll never forget you. Ever."

"He was my first new friend," I say to Jenny.

"Mine too," she chokes.

"He wanted us..." I gulp down a sob and Jenny squeezes my hand.

She nods her head. "I know."

I think of the day I saw him in the zoo. "Find a new private place wherever you are," I say to him. "A safe spot where no one will watch you. Where there's no senseless noise."

The irony makes me grimace as the sound of chaos fills the air. I hug his lifeless body. My chest feels hollow, and my body aches.

"We have to go," Jenny's mom says as she pulls my listless arm.

"We can't leave him," Jenny pleads.

"We have no choice," her mom says, scanning the sky. Now I hear the noise that made her look up. The sound of Governcorp helicopters. "We have to go," she repeats.

"His glasses," Jenny screams. "Over there." She points a few feet away, and Kyle hands them to her. "He can't be without his glasses," she whispers as she places them on his face.

The helicopters are near and low in the sky. They're shooting smoke in the air. Jenny's mom yanks us both away from Russell, but we just stand staring at him. Suddenly, my eyes burn from the tear gas, and my throat closes so tightly I feel suffocated.

"Go. Go!" Jenny's mom yells fiercely. Her voice jolts me and although my heart feels numb, the will to survive moves my legs faster than I can imagine. My dad grabs Kyle's arm to help him limp as fast as possible down the street away from the grandstand and helicopters. Jenny's mom speeds ahead, and I can barely keep her in sight.

I strip off my clown shirt and use it to block my nose and mouth. My eyes water so much it's hard to see. I trip on horns and drums and souvenirs abandoned in the street as I race to keep up. People run in all directions and yell names to find others lost in the chaos. My ears hurt from the high-pitched, eerie sounds coming from Broadcasters that aren't receiving signals. But the worst of it all is the barrage of sound from Protectors everywhere, and the screams of the wounded.

We run down three long blocks. We're all panting, especially my dad. My eyes hurt so much I want to scream, but Jenny's mom won't let us stop.

"We only have twelve minutes," she says leading us.

"What happens in twelve minutes?" Jenny asks.

Her mom points up the hill ahead. "We need to go up there."

This part of the hill might be the steepest in the city, and it's mostly rocks and dirt without much grass.

"Up this way? Why?" Jenny asks the question we're all thinking.

"We need to get to North Street unseen."

"Why?" Jenny asks again.

"Up. Up. Go!" her mom screams.

Jenny

Now Hannah helps Kyle, and we all follow my mom. There are no paths, just rocks to trip on and holes to fall in. A few drops of rain splat the dirt. I can't figure out what my mom is doing. Why are we climbing this horrible hill when we can't breathe from the gas in our lungs? Is there a place to hide up there?

Halfway up, Kyle moans in pain and then falls, and my mom has no choice but to let us stop for a minute. We're high enough to see smoke from blocks away. Something is on fire.

"It's the Homestead," Hannah gasps. Her dad hugs her and makes her turn away. I want to say something, but I don't know the right thing to say. I reach into my pocket and pull out Shirazu. Hannah shoves him in her pocket without a glance. He's let her down. I hug her, but there's nothing more I can do.

Kyle moans again. "Do you want me to retie your bandage?" I ask.

He shakes his head. He hasn't said anything to me since he got off the float.

"Do you believe me? That I'm sorry?" I ask.

"Sure," he says flatly.

My stomach sinks and my throat tightens.

"Let's go!" my mom yells, and I hurry behind her.

"Jenny, it's your turn!" Hannah calls to me.

I grab Kyle's arm without looking at him. We climb in silence. My arm hurts, my legs hurt, my whole body hurts. Rain hits my face, and I'm glad because I can wipe tears away without being obvious.

"I just saw the kindest person I will ever know die," I say. "I may die too, but I want you to know that you are the only boy I ever liked and I'm sorry I ruined it."

Kyle is quiet for a minute, struggling to put weight on his injured leg as the rocks slide under us in the rain. "You didn't believe me," he says at last.

"Never mind," I say.

"You didn't believe me that I like you," he says.

"You were nice because you thought I could help you."

"I was nice because I wanted to be nice," Kyle says.

"I know Jade gave you notes," I say.

"Yeah," he says. "And I wrote one back that said leave me alone."

"Hurry!" my mom yells. I feel my chest cave and a new emptiness in my stomach. I'm not sure if I can move. I'm not sure if I want to. I messed everything up again. My knees beg to give way. I've dropped Kyle's arm—I can't remember how. I turn into the hill and wish I could disappear. I feel Kyle limp closer. He takes my hand, and I turn around. He locks eyes with me and pulls me towards him, then reaches around my waist, and kisses me. It's gentle and caring and lasts just a second. He smiles. Without hesitation, I put my arms around his neck, and even though my eyes are closed, my mouth finds his like magic. We push our lips together much harder this time. His lips are full and soft. I feel the hammer of my heart and butterflies in my stomach.

It's everything I hoped it would be.

Hannah

I watch Jenny and Kyle kiss. I smile even though I feel a pang in my heart. Where are you, Jonah? Jenny's mom gives another order for us to hurry as she sprints toward the top of the hill.

"Don't leave us!" Jenny hollers, but her mom disappears over the crest.

The rain is steady, and I use the water to wipe my face and get rid of my clown makeup. I can look like my old self, but how will I ever *be* my old self again?

The rocks are slippery, and the dirt has become a mud that sucks our feet like cement. Each step is more challenging than the one before. We help each other climb, but without Jenny's mom yelling at us, we are slow, cautious, and uninspired.

I turn and stop at the slightest sound.

"Keep going," Kyle says.

"What was that noise?" I ask.

"Nothing," he says. "Don't think. Just keep going."

Don't think. Don't think. All the thoughts to avoid flood my head. Where are my mom and sisters? Are they even alive? Where is Maria and everyone else I know?

"Did you know about that group in the float?" I ask.

Kyle shakes his head, no.

"Do you think Jonah…?"

"We only know what our group planned."

This wasn't the question on my mind. I look away. Maybe it's better not to ask.

"Hey…" Kyle touches my arm, then searches for some words. "If anyone can… if anyone can escape." He nods his head trying to assure me.

"There was so much shooting by the float," I say.

"Huh? He wasn't on the float."

I stop mid-stride and stare at Kyle. "What?"

"He programmed all that ahead of time in case…in case."

A woman's scream pierces the air, and we all freeze. The sound is so sorrowful that my own body feels pain. Or maybe it's the pain of thinking Jonah may still be in the Comfort Center or worse; the "in case" scenario. I close my eyes and lean against a rock.

My dad takes my arm gently. He's soaked to the bone in his t-shirt and pants. "We're almost there," he says.

It's laughable how he says it. "Almost there," as if a transformed universe–the world of Oz–is just over the hilltop.

Almost where? And then what?

Jenny

I pant as I get to the top. I recognize where we are. North Street–across from Buy Now. Are we going to hide there? Why did my mom make us come here? I just want to lie down and collapse and be with her. But she's nowhere.

I'm shaking so much my teeth chatter.

Kyle takes my hand and puts his arm around me. "We'll be okay," he says.

The tingling I feel from his fingers entwined with mine makes me want to believe him.

The Buy Now alarm is blasting as people go in and out of the broken store windows, stealing whatever they can carry. A Broadcaster crackles to life above us.

Official Report: Thank you, citizens, for keeping your friends and family safe. Our wonderful Comfort Center personnel will help everyone who is sick. Use Protectors against criminals.

I want to scream, but I bury my head on Kyle's shoulder instead. Flakeman is gone but not the lies.

"There's your mom!" Hannah yells.

She comes out of an alley between two apartment buildings. She stops and takes off her safety officer jacket, and then throws it in a trashcan. I feel a knot in my stomach. It's over. Our old life–my old goals–my old plans. They're gone forever.

"No one down there," my mom mumbles when she reaches us. She seems puzzled, but isn't that a good thing? No one there to shoot us?

She hugs me tightly.

"I'm scared," I say.

"I know," she says.

We hug again. I think of my question to Hannah, "How can you tell what's real?" I'm so glad I know this is.

My mom looks at Kyle and his bandaged leg. "I'm sorry I did that," she says.

Before he can say anything, we hear the roar of another helicopter. On the sidewalk like this, officials could shoot us easily and not waste more tear gas.

"Hide!" I yell. But there's no time. The helicopter painted with the Governcorp logo soars right at us. It's huge. A military vehicle with three propellers. Everyone but my mom ducks down and covers their head as it flies over our heads and then past us.

"Stay together," my mom says.

I look around for a good place to hide. Shouldn't we run? Why isn't my mom telling us what to do?

The helicopter comes out of the clouds again and shines a light beam down on our group. I reach to clutch my mom, but she darts for the Buy Now parking lot.

"MOM!"

Kyle grabs me before I can race after her.

Hannah

Jenny screams, but her mom keeps going. The helicopter turns the light away and hovers over the Buy Now parking lot. People holding Protectors run out from a different alley farther down the street and head right for us. I grab onto my dad's arm. Who will attack us first?

"We've got to run!" I yell to my dad over the helicopter roar.

He shakes his head and points to Jenny's mom. Now she's scrambling toward the other group.

The helicopter fights to stay level as thunder and lightening fill the air and the rain comes down harder. The machine rocks with an unnatural motion and then swings too far to the right, and a propeller hits a viewer pole. The helicopter shakes and whines as the propeller chops at the metal pole. It makes a sickly whir like a blender about to break from strain. It swings to the side again, and I put my arm in front of my face, anticipating a horrible crash, but instead, it jolts up into the sky like a rocket. It circles for a minute and then descends back toward the parking lot.

Something drops from the middle of the machine.

A ladder? Who wants us on board? The rope swings wildly from side to side, rising and falling with the unsteady machine and blustering wind. Someone from the other group lunges toward the ladder, grabs on, and climbs up like an expert.

After several minutes, the helicopter steadies. It lowers to a level even with the Buy Now roof, and the rope hangs much straighter and stiller. The people in the other group climb up one by one.

Jenny's mom runs back to us. "You can climb up, right?" she says to Kyle.

"Which side are you on?" he asks.

"I just want to protect people," she says.

He still looks suspicious, but Jenny grabs Kyle's hand, and they follow her mom.

I look at my dad and shake my head. "What about Mom? Lily? Emma?"

"She'll help us find them," my dad answers.

"How do you know?" I ask. "We're climbing into a Governcorp helicopter."

"I trust her," he says.

Trust your head or your heart? What about Jonah? I look at my dad's hopeful face, and I reluctantly let him lead me to the rope ladder. What other choice do I really have?

"I'll go last," Jenny's mom says as she holds the rope.

"No," Jenny insists. "You and Mr. Cossack are stronger to help Kyle. You go first and put Kyle in-between."

It's a better plan. Jenny's mom hesitates, but when the sound of Governcorp sirens reach us, she steps up on the ladder.

"Right after us," she orders. "Right. After."

Jenny nods, and we watch the three awkwardly climb. After a few slips, they get into a rhythm that creeps them toward the top.

I look over at Buy Now and think of the many hiding spots inside. I could wait until it's safe and make my way back home and find my mom and sisters. I hear Jonah's voice in my head, "*Do the right thing*." I glance up. Kyle and the others are almost at the opening. What is the right thing?

The Broadcaster comes on. The words are muffled by the roar of the helicopter, but I don't need to hear them to know what they encourage: fanciful thinking, blind acceptance, walking away from the truth.

I feel my teeth clench, and I sprint towards the Broadcaster.

"Hannah!" Jenny screams and then chases after me.

I get to the Broadcaster and pull Shizaru from my pocket along with my other figurine of the three monkeys. *See no evil. Hear no evil. Speak no evil. Do no evil.*

It's almost enough, but not quite.

"What are you doing?" Jenny yells. "We have to go! NOW!"

I place my monkeys on top of the vile box. I think about what Jenny's mom said to Kyle. Protecting people means doing something. Kyle, Jonah, Maria, Zora, Russell–all understood that nothing changes without action. Even the zoo monkeys understood. Now I know it, too.

"I'm staying," I yell to Jenny. "I have to fight."

"Not by yourself," she screams. "Don't you think, I'm fighting too?" she says as she grabs my arm. I want to shake her off, but what she says next makes me cling to her instead. "After what happened to Russell, I will never stop fighting. *We* will never stop until things change."

She looks into my eyes and after a few moments, I nod in agreement.

Jenny grabs my hand, and we run back to the dangling rope. I climb onto the first step, and Jenny taps me on the leg and points up. Jonah has on his old beret. He holds a large, white placard like any chauffeur would. In the boldest letters possible it reads, Hannah.

Jenny

We climb as close to side by side as the rope will allow. My head is filled with questions. Where are we going? How many protesters are there? Are Homesteads burning all over the country? How many citizens are fighting for change?

I'm not afraid of questions anymore.

We see the billows of smoke from the Homestead. I almost ask Hannah, "Which side do you think did it?" but I know it doesn't matter. Answers are never easy. A Protector saved my life. A Protector killed Russell. Opportunity people can become citizens. Opportunity people are trapped in Homesteads. If one person is right, is the other person wrong? I smile as the word enters my brain. *Conundrum.*

We're a step away from the helicopter opening. I can see a huge billboard ad for Protectors posted on a building far away. The Protector picture has been ripped off, and all that's left are the words that mean so much more than I ever could imagine.

Together We Are Strong.

I squeeze Hannah's hand as we step into the helicopter and lift into the air.

FOR WHAT IT'S WORTH

There's something happening here
What it is ain't exactly clear
There's a man with a gun over there
Telling me I got to beware

I think it's time we stop, children, what's that sound
Everybody look what's going down

There's battle lines being drawn
Nobody's right if everybody's wrong
Young people speaking their minds
Getting so much resistance from behind

It's time we stop, hey, what's that sound
Everybody look what's going down

What a field-day for the heat
A thousand people in the street
Singing songs and carrying signs
Mostly say, hooray for our side

It's time we stop, hey, what's that sound
Everybody look what's going down

Paranoia strikes deep
Into your life it will creep
It starts when you're always afraid
You step out of line, the man come and take you away

We better stop, hey, what's that sound
Everybody look what's going down
Stop, hey, what's that sound
Everybody look what's going down

Stop, now, what's that sound
Everybody look what's going down
Stop, children, what's that sound
Everybody look what's going down

FOR WHAT IT'S WORTH
Words and Music by STEPHEN STILLS
Copyright © 1967 (Renewed)
COTILLION MUSIC INC., TEN EAST MUSIC
SPRINGFIELD TOONES AND RICHIE FURAY MUSIC
All Rights Administrated by
WARNER-TAMERLANE PUBLISHING CORP.
All rights Reserved
Used by Permission of ALFRED MUSIC

Acknowledgements

Thanks to Michael Erickson and David Crespy for their support in the development of the play, Four Wise Monkeys, upon which this book is based. Thanks to all the theatre producers who enjoyed the play and especially those who suggested it could be a young adult novel.

Thanks to Martha Schuller, Mary Ann Cook, and Angelle Pilkington for their contributions to the editing.

Thanks to all the friends who read various drafts especially Gailya, Bryna, Ann, Pat, Savitri, Lucy, Lois, Lillian, Floss, Susan, Marcia, Rebecca, and Jill for commenting on early versions. A special thanks to Lauren, Annelise, and Mitali for taking time to read an early version and providing valuable feedback.

Finally, and most importantly, love and thanks to Jim, Rachel, and Hannah for supporting and encouraging all my creative efforts. Hannah, you keep me inspired!

About the Author

Joël Doty is a proud graduate of University of Michigan, Temple University and Northeastern Illinois University. She is a playwright and her play, Four Wise Monkeys, written in 2009, is the foundation for this story. This is her first novel.